The Monstrous Child

About the Author

Francesca Simon is universally known for the staggeringly popular *Horrid Henry* series. These books and CDs have sold over 20 million copies in the UK alone and are published in 27 countries. *Horrid Henry and the Abominable Snowman* won the Children's Book of the the Year award in 2008. She has also published two middle-grade novels: *The Lost Gods* and *The Sleeping Army*. Francesca lives in London with her family. This is her first teen novel.

About the Illustrator

Olivia Lomenech Gill lives and works in Northumberland. Originally trained in theatre, Olivia has worked as a professional artist for over a decade. As a printmaker Olivia has won several awards and her work has been exhibited at the Royal Academy. She was shortlisted for the Kate Greenaway Medal for her work on *Where My Wellies Take Me* by Michael Morpurgo, which was her first book illustration project.

ALSO BY FRANCESCA SIMON

The Lost Gods

The Sleeping Army

THE HORRID HENRY SERIES

Higgledy Piggledy the Hen Who Loved to Dance

Helping Hercules

Papa Forgot

Do You Speak English, Moon?

Hugo and the Bullyfrogs

Three Cheers for Ostrich

What's That Noise?

Don't Wake the Baby

Spider School

The Topsy Turvies

The Haunted House of Buffin Street

Moo Baa Baa Quack

Don't Cook Cinderella

FRANCESCA SIMON

With illuminations by Olivia Lomenech Gill

ff
FABER & FABER

P
PROFILE BOOKS

First published in the UK in 2016
First published in the USA in 2017
by Faber & Faber Limited
Bloomsbury House,
74–77 Great Russell Street,
London WC1B 3DA
and
Profile Books
3 Holford Yard, Bevin Way,
London WC1X 9HD
www.profilebooks.com
This paperback edition first published in 2017

Typeset by M Rules
Printed by CPI Group (UK) Ltd, Croydon CR0 4YY

A CIP record for this book
is available from the British Library

ISBN 978-0-571-33027-0

4 6 8 10 9 7 5 3

For my son, Joshua

As far from monstrous as it is possible to be

CONTENTS

The sunflowers weave a golden clime,
As though their season had no date,
Nod to the iron shoes of Time,
And play with his immortal hate.

W. B. YEATS

PART 1
Jotunheim

I

CORPSE BABY

OU'D THINK AFTER my brother the snake was born they'd have stopped at one. But no.

Next was the wolf, Fenrir.

And then me.

How Mum must have hoped, when my top half slithered out, that it was third time lucky. A human head. Praise the Blood Mother. Pink cheeks. Pale skin. No scales! Two arms. Ten little fingers at the end of two dimpled hands. Oh, thank you Blood Mother, thank you Hekla the fierce one, Earth Spewer, Ancestors all. Finally, finally, I am blessed. Oh, sound the horns, bang the drums. My darling, my baby, my beauty, almost there.

Panting. Straining. Pushing. A little god? A little goddess? Who cared, just so long as –

And then slither. *Plop.* Out I come, dangling my rotting legs. Corpse baby. Carrion tot. The third monster.

Mum screamed. Cursed the Earth Spewer and the Sun Swallower.

Dad – well, Dad probably would have screamed too, if he'd been around. Which he wasn't.

And me? Yeah, I screamed. Everyone else was – why shouldn't I join the party?

I slipped from her hands and smacked onto the rocky ground. Ouch. Ow. Mum kept on screaming and wailing.

I remember everything. I remember it all.

What's she howling about? I thought. *I'm the one flopped on the floor.*

Then rough grey fur. Growling.

A tongue licked me. I flinched. Fen's iron breath chilling my face. That's fitting, isn't it, that my first smell is putrid.

'Leave it, Fenrir,' said Mum. (Thanks, Mum!) She tossed my wolf brother a bloody haunch of meat. He tore into it with frantic whimperings. I heard the hideous squelchy sound of raw flesh being ripped from bone.

Mum looked down at me, then turned away. Her tears dribbled onto my face.

It's not all about you, Mum. What do you think it's like for me? Okay, I didn't think that then. I'm a goddess, but even I was born a mewling infant.

I lay naked on my back and looked up at the rocky ceiling, black with smoke. This is my cold, dark, noisy, heavy world. Screaming. Slobbering. Could be worse. Could be better. What did I know then?

Each of you must endure the ending of life in this world.

But not me.

Time's iron feet don't trample over me. Time is what I

have. Time without end. A long, dull, everlasting eternity. I live in time and out of time. Time for me stands still.

I am Hel, Goddess of the Dead.

This is my story. This is my word-shrine. This is my testament. I don't know who will be alive to hear it, but I want to tell my saga. For too long others have spoken for me; now I speak for myself.

I wasn't always lying silent and rotting on a stinking bed in the Underworld. Listening to snakes hissing and corpses shrieking.

I am telling about the time before time, when Midgard was new and shiny and unpeopled, Asgard was half built and the gods settling into their kingdom, drawing boundaries, establishing their cruel dominion over the rest of us.

I didn't start off hating everything.

I liked flowers.

I liked trees.

I liked mountains.

I liked glaciers.

It was just mortals I couldn't stand. And the gods. And my family.

Oh.

Just one more thing. Before you reject me, before you hate me, remember: I never asked to be Hel's queen.

2

BAD BLOOD

O WHAT DO YOU need to know about my rancid family?

My mother was a giantess. My father was a god. The gods are on top. Number one. Top dogs. Pack leaders. Goddesses are number two. All giants are far, far beneath them. Muck on their shoes.

But lots of gods marry giantesses, have children with giantesses. Happens all the time. No one thinks anything of it. Gods can do whatever they like.

In fact, Odin's mother was a giantess. So when Odin gets all high and mighty, and refers to the gods as *The Sacred People*, and giants as so much vermin good only for building walls and having their heads bashed in, you just remember all that giant blood coursing in what he likes to think of as his godly veins.

The god Frey's wife was a giantess. Thor's mother, Jord, was – no prizes for guessing but you got it – a giantess. Are we starting to see a little pattern here? The great giant-killer, the great skull-smasher Thor, is half giant himself. He was probably braining his cousins and aunties with his hateful hammer without even realising it.

But *goddesses* do not, I repeat, *do not*, fall in love with giants or have children with giants.

Until one did.

Yup. My grandmother. My father's mother. (Thanks, Gran.)

Granny Laufey was a goddess (keep up). Skinny

and bony, so she was nicknamed Nal the Needle. Mum always spat when she said her name.

'Nal's not coming near you,' said Mum. 'Stuck-up sow. I can't bear the way she looks down on me. I never asked for Loki's attentions. She can stick to her own and leave us be.'

Got that? It's important. Loki's *mother*, my granny, was a *goddess* and his *father* was a *giant*. Oops. Wrong way round. WRONG. WRONG. WRONG. Because then whose side are you on? The gods? Or the giants? You're betwixt and between. Children are always meant to follow their father's clan. My grandmother's lapse made Dad an enemy within Asgard. Take a bow, Granny.

What's that saying? Better to have your enemy inside the tent pissing out, then outside pissing in.

Doesn't always work.

So let's get this straight, once and for all.

If your dad's a GOD and your mum's a GIANTESS – good. That's how it should be. Welcome to Asgard and here's your gleaming hall. Just look at that stuck-up giantess Gerd when she flounced off to marry the god Frey. They couldn't open the Asgard gates fast enough for her and her wealth.

But . . .

If your *dad's* a GIANT and your *mum's* a GODDESS – bad.

In fact very bad. Bad. Bad. Bad. Bad. Bad.

So bad it only happened once.

And so my fate was sealed. I had bad blood. Bad blood from my mother. Worse blood from my dad. Can't really argue with that. I mean, just look at my brothers.

3

I AM NAMED

OU STILL WITH ME? Good. Hang in there – it's worth the journey. Just think of all those foolish mortals who try to unearth the secrets of the dead, and lucky you – you get them without risking your life sneaking down beneath the World Tree before your days and deeds are finished.

So where was I? I'm born, I'm naked, I'm lying on the

freezing ground looking up into frightened faces. I'm cold and angry. All around me I hear wailing. But I'm quiet. Even then, I wasn't one to make a fuss. There's an awful smell, sweet and foul.

The wolf cub sniffed me, then snarled. I tried to move my legs, my black feeble legs, which barely budge, my hands curled into red fists. Mum kicked him away. I doubt I looked good enough to eat, but with Fen you never knew.

Fen howled. Hard to believe, but he was like a puppy then. A puppy with big, slashing teeth, but still ... You could pretend he was just playing. That he didn't mean it when he ripped open your face.

My other brother, Jormungand, slithered over to me and hissed. He always scared me, my brother the snake. Even now those words are horrible to write ... my brother the snake.

Mum, screaming, kicks him away too. Stomp on his head, Mum! Go on, you can do it. That would have saved so much fuss and bother. But no. Jor lands smack on the table. Bowls and cups and drinking horns fly everywhere. Fenrir snarls at Jor, hackles up, jaws dripping. Jor bares his fangs, spitting poison. The two of them, always spitting and fighting. Always eyeing me, as if I were a hunk of carrion they'd like to devour.

Have you gathered how much I hate my brothers?

Hiss. Growl. Hiss. Growl. Hiss. Growl. Amazing I learned to talk, really, with the conversation that went on around me.

Hello! Is no one going to pick me up?

Nope. Seems not.

I remember the cave filling with visitors. They were frosty and snow-covered, stamping their feet and shaking out their sleet-heavy cloaks, spraying slush everywhere. Someone, not Mum, finally lifted me with their icy chapped hands and I was swaddled in furs, only my top half on show. My mother huddled in the corner, rocking back and forth on her haunches.

'Angrboda. What a pretty baby.'

Oh, how nice. Who said that?

Great. It's Dad's brother. My *blind* uncle, Helblindi. Compliments from a blind god. Brilliant. He's standing next to my father, Loki (hi, Dad! Glad you could make the party), who is definitely wishing he wasn't here and pretending he has nothing to do with any of this.

My mother's grey eyes flash. She's fierce, my mother. You do not want to mess with her.

'Unwrap it,' she says. Pokes me with a stick.

The cave is suddenly silent.

A troll picks at my swaddling with her flabby hand and holds up a torch. I hear her suck in her breath and step back. The troll behind her screams. Another sway-backed ogre, his nose broken with huge twisted knots like the horns of old rams, skulks off on his bent knees.

What? Even a *troll* recoils from me?

Who are you, you ugly troll, to scream at the sight of me? Am I so hideous, so revolting, that the foulest creatures alive can't bear to look? What am I?

Loki turns away. 'Kill it,' he says.

'You let the others live. Why start now?' says Uncle.

'It's half corpse,' says Dad.

'She's a goddess. She won't die easily,' says Uncle.

Dad hesitates. I start to cry.

Can we just pause here for a minute? My dad wants me killed. And Mum isn't even lifting her head. It's the father's choice, if the baby lives or dies. But come on, Mum. Defend me. Protect me.

No? Nothing?

I try to kick off the rest of my swaddling. Why don't my legs obey me? They feel weak and wavery, as if they are part of me, but somehow not.

'Have it your own way,' says Dad.

Yay. I get to live. I seem to be the only one who's happy about this.

My mother raises her head. She doesn't touch me.

Loki shrugs and sprinkles water on me. My uncle names me Hel. It means *to cover*. Stupid name, but believe me it could have been so much worse. I could have been called Blood Hair, or Dung Heap, or Mud Face. Giants don't give great names. My own mother

Angrboda's name means *distress-bringer.* What was my grandpa thinking? Who'd name their own wee girl *Distress-Bringer* and bury anguish in her name? It's almost as if you're asking for trouble. You're sprinkling the naming water on the screaming brat, and calling on the Fates to bring misery. Isn't there enough sorrow in the worlds without seeking it? You're shaking your fists at the Fates and shouting, 'Yoo hoo, ladies, look down, do your worst.'

And boy did they ever.

But I am leaping ahead. It's hard for me to think in a line like you fate-bound ones.

Dad didn't lift me on his knee after he sprinkled water on me and Uncle spoke my name. There was a murmuring. Mum snatched me instead.

Look, Mum! No claws or scales. Be grateful for what you have.

'Let's see it again,' said Dad.

Again with the *it*.

Angrboda unwrapped me.

'Uhhh,' he said, recoiling. He held his nose. 'Disgusting.'

Mum dipped her drinking horn into Hymir's brewing cauldron, which he had supplied for my birth feast, and hurled the mead in his face.

'Leave me and the monsters.'

Dad grabbed her hair.

'I'll leave when I'm ready.'

Mum shook herself free. 'She's yours,' she hissed. 'Like it or not.'

4

WHO HASN'T MET A GIANT WITH THREE HEADS?

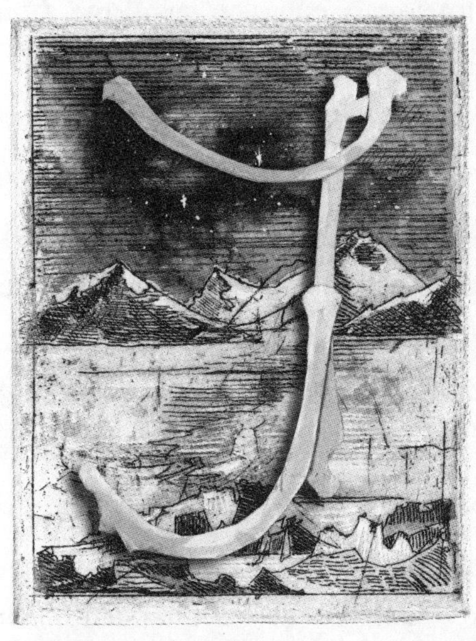

OTUNHEIM, MY FROST world, lies east of Asgard. Girdled with snow and sleet and ice, the wind roars, whipping the blasted trees and piling up snow in drifts against the cliffs. My iron-grey home.

If only our mountain realm had been further out of reach of the slippery gods, I might have been safer. But it was as if they couldn't leave us alone. Thor came to bash in our heads with his murderous hammer; others came to steal our gold. (We create nothing from precious ore, that's what dwarves are for, but we like its glitter and shine, the cool weight in our hands.)

The gods have always invaded our land seeking wisdom or looking for love. Yeah, you heard me. Can we smash right now the myth that giants are all hideous, ignorant brutes? Anyone who *thinks* giants are the lowest of the low has been spending too much time believing the lying, thieving gods.

Giants lived countless winters before the gods raised up the corners of the earth and formed the heavens. We witnessed what happened, and we kept the sacred lore. Where do you think the gods went to get their knowledge of the past and the future?

Yup. From us.

Where did One-Eyed Odin get his skill in poetry? No prizes – that smooth-tongued, deceiving god STOLE THE MEAD OF POETRY FROM GIANTS! Obviously we weren't using it – we had better things to do than spew poetry – but it was ours. A few drops spilled as One-Eye made his cowardly escape, from which mortals, unfortunately, learned to compose their twanging verses, hoping for fame. One of the absurd reasons gods think they're so much better than giants is that One-Eye bores everyone senseless reciting great screeds of the stuff. Even mortals get in on the act, yowling and rhyming away.

Poetry. What a waste of time. And *you* don't have time to waste, even if I have an eternityful.

You mortals have so many wrong ideas about giants. For some reason you think *all* giants are gigantic.

Hello?

The *old* ones from whom we get our name were huge. The ones who created the mountains by hurling rocks, and islands when they dropped earth from their aprons while fording the seas. But most of us are the same stature as the gods.

Taller than mortals, obviously, but that's it.

Nor are we all thick.

There are brainless giants and clever giants. What? In which group am I? One thing I will say for Loki's children, we didn't get whacked with the stupid stick. Whereas the ugly stick – yes, I'd say I was beaten long and hard with it.

True, we mountain-dwellers, we rock-dwellers, weren't all specimens of beauty. The god Tyr's granny was a giantess with 900 heads. So what? It happens. (He escaped lightly, inheriting just the one.) And who hasn't met a giant with three or six heads? But we weren't *all* hideous and deformed brutes, whatever the gods say. We weren't all fire demons and flesh-eating monsters. My mother was beautiful. You think Dad would've hightailed after some hag?

Forgive me for getting a little overheated there. Few things make me angry any more. But I don't like hearing my ancestors insulted and I can't abide the lies.

The victor writes the saga.

Remember that.

5

UNWRAP THE BANDAGES

S A CHILD I NEVER smiled. Ever. Or laughed. Not even when Fen got up on his hind legs and danced before biting a rat in half.

What exactly did I have to smile about?

I once heard a story about a rich giantess who would only marry the giant who made her laugh. She'd chop off the heads of the ones who didn't. That would be me, surrounded by skulls.

My nature is sombre and fierce. That's who I am, not some jolly skipping elf, beaming and twining daisies to crown my golden locks. My hair is silver, by the way. Coiling and curling past my shoulders. Strong like a fishing line. My hair is the only part of me others want to pat and pull. I hate being touched so no one dares, but I can see it in their faces. I tried to comb it once, with my mother's comb, and the walrus ivory splintered. She walloped me for that. Maybe Dad gave her the comb (unlikely – Dad wasn't exactly lavish with gifts). I can't see why she made such a fuss. I thought, Why do you beat me? Get another comb. Who cares, it's just a comb. She's the mother of a snake and a wolf and a half-corpse, you'd think she'd have more serious stuff to get upset about.

I rarely went outside. I hated being shouted at as I lurched around on my corpse legs, wind-blown and bent over in the hail, my ice-white hair shrouding my face, hoping no one would notice me.

Fat chance.

‘Aren’t you the lovely one?’ said a two-headed troll, smacking his rubbery lips.

Compliments from a troll.

It was easier just to stay hidden in our cave.

When I say ‘cave’, I’m exaggerating. Did you imagine I lived in a dank pit like some ogre? Underground like a dwarf in a furnace? Ha. Our cave was more like a great hall than some low hole. Remember who’s talking to you. Hel. I’m a goddess.

Unfortunately (a word bound to me with iron fetters), wherever I shuffle about in our cave the smell hits me. Heavy. Foul. Overlaid with the perfume of rancid wet dog (thanks, Fen) and anything noxious and maggotty he’d dragged home from Ironwood on which to snack.

And then, of course, there was me. I brought my own stink with me wherever I went. We kept a smoking lamp, filled with oils, to mask the odour but it never did.

We’ve been avoiding the subject. Let’s take a look at my bottom half, shall we? You know you want to. Go on, have a good gape at my carrion legs. I’ll lift up my furs and unwrap the bandages, set aside the rosemary and mint I use to try to hide my stench. What colour will my twisted legs be today? How much more decayed the flesh? They moulder and stink, blotched with gangrene. And yet they never rot away: corpse legs suspended in life. My immortal flesh never peels off. It just stays attached, reeking and putrefying.

And what about my face? What about it? I have two eyes, a nose, a mouth. Do you really think anyone gets close enough to me to take a second look? One whiff and they're off.

Seen enough? Smelled enough?

Sometimes I dream my legs are whole. I run, or fly, I move gracefully through the worlds. Then I wake and I'm back to my monstrous self, jerking like a cart with a broken wheel. Walking is hard for me. I spend a lot of time lying on my mat or sitting on a cushioned chair, a bearskin pulled over my legs. I watch the slaves gut fish and hang it to dry on racks by the fire. (Yes, of course we had slaves. We weren't savages. They fetched firewood and water, fed and cleaned the animals, made butter and cheese, brewed ale and mead. Occasionally one of them would unwrap my bandages and wrap my corpse legs in fresh ones – as if new cloth could make any difference.)

My father visits every so often, but then I'm banished immediately. He picks Fen up by the scruff of his neck and hurls him out of the cave. Jor slithers away before he can be caught. I move towards him –

'Go away! You stink of death. My gods,' he'd yell, before sweeping my mother up in his arms. Mum is kinder when Dad's not around. When he is, I might as well be a fish bone.

I remember huddling on the floor while Mum and Dad screamed and hurled benches and platters. Once Dad smashed a plate of food to the floor, which no one touched for nights. Even Fen left it alone. And I thought, *Just go away, Dad. We don't need you. Just go away.*

When they fought, it was easier for Fen and Jor to scuttle out. I couldn't really move, so I hid, made myself small. Dad cursed Mum for breeding monsters.

She cursed him for siring us. 'Trolls take you!' they screeched at each other.

I would take cover under a bench, humming oh so quietly to myself, sending my thoughts far away. I'd heard that two of the goddesses had falcon capes that gave them wings to fly and I wished with all my heart I had one too.

When it was just Mum and us, which was more and more often, what can I say? Once she made a rattle of bones for me. I clacked them together a few times, more in shock because I'd been given a toy. Then I dropped it and Fen chomped it up. Mum never made me another. Actually, I didn't need any noisemakers. What with the hissing and the howling and the fighting and the shouting, there was enough noise to fill the cave without me adding a few rattles of my own.

I've heard there are parents who smother their children with love. Give them the choicest tidbits. Wrap them in the softest furs. Tickle them under the chin and call them 'dumpling' and 'honey lamb'.

Ugh. I can't imagine that.

6

LAST SUPPER

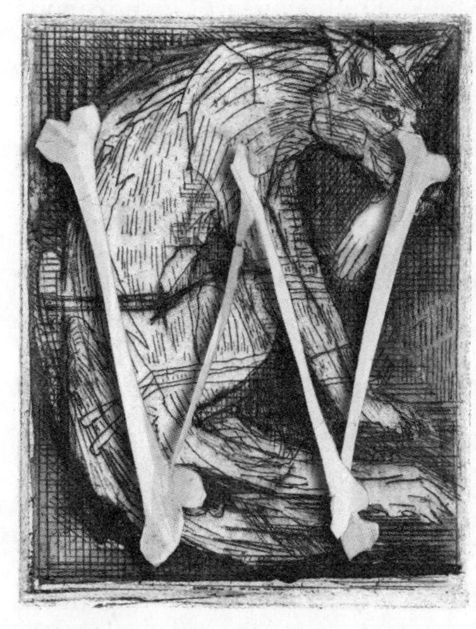

E'RE COMING TO THE end of my miserable life in Jotunheim (what? So soon?). It was a golden time of enchanted beauty compared to what followed. Let's drop in at the last supper, bid a final farewell and good riddance to the monstrous family.

Fen is asleep, snarling with his gravel growl. His legs shake.

'He's dreaming of savaging sheep,' said Mum. She was a seeress for all the good that power did her. (And, no, I'm not sharing her charms with you. What, and have everyone chanting away, raising the dead, demanding knowledge? I shudder just thinking about it.)

I can still see Mum sitting by the fire draped in her wolf pelts, their tails dangling over her shoulder, her hair twisted and tumbling, the colour of wet earth. When she'd let me, I liked to play with the skinned heads, inventing little conversations. She is gripping a bloody wolfskin in her teeth, cleaning and scraping the hide with a sharp stone. The scratching sound always made me shiver. She'd attach the skins round her waist with my favourite carved bone in the shape of a bear claw. Some dwarf must have made it for her – giants don't carve anything.

Wolf bones lie scattered around her, tufted with flecks of flesh and sinewy with muscle. Fen darts up to grab the bones, then retreats to his bearskin, gnawing and chewing.

Slaves fill the stone lamps with fish oil and light them, clogging the cave with smoke. A cauldron is bubbling. Fish and apples on the table, soup in bowls, mead in cups. Like all gods, I don't *need* to eat, but we do it for pleasure. Mum and I are sitting on benches at the table, my troll-tempered brothers scrabbling around and eating off the floor, growling and hissing.

I can hear ravens cawing *kraa kraa kraa* as they circle above the forest, and the wolves in Ironwood howling, more like the screaming of corpses than any living thing. It's a comfort being inside, deep in our cave, listening to evil creatures shrieking at the edge of night as they seek prey other than you.

The High Seat is empty, in case Dad should drop by. Talk about hope over experience. The damp walls glisten and the shrines are laden with offerings to our ancestors, Blood Mother, Volcano Father, Mountain Crusher and Earth Spewer. The daily sacrifice of fresh meat is laid out, to keep the ancestors sweet, and Mum has intoned the charms. The Old Ones stir and rumble when they're ignored.

So what's spoiling the happy suppertime scene? Yes, you got it, having to eat with a drooling wolf and a poisonous snake.

Fenrir tears apart joints of deer meat, swallowing in great gulps, bone, gristle, flesh. Then he licks the blood from his jaw. Jor prefers mice. Luckily our cave was full of them. His snaky body is lumpy with vermin.

But let's move our disgusted gaze off the ground and up to the table and benches, and pretend my brothers aren't there.

Sitting at the table was my favourite thing. The table hides my lower body. Protects me from horrified eyes. Sitting there, barely tall enough to see above the top, resting my plump arms on the scratched wood for balance, I look for a few moments like the goddess that I am. If you were to walk in – and not get torn to pieces by my brothers – you'd think I was just a fair young goddess sharing a mead horn with her, to be honest, far, far better looking mother. Sometimes I wonder what that was like for her, such a beauty, to give birth to . . . us.

My monstrous brothers scrabble about on the floor, brawling over rats.

'Stop fighting!' Mum screams. 'Or bloody Thor with his hammer will come smash your skulls.' That shut them up – for a moment. Even Fen and Jor don't like the giant-killer's hammer mentioned.

But *I'm* at the table. Eating with a knife. I'm never forced to eat on the ground. It means I am different from the beasts. Better. More like Mum. I sit up straight. I am careful not to slurp. Anything to make Mum like me, just a little. I give Mum a little present of carved bone – I have no talent; it was awful, pathetic scratchings on walrus tusk, which she looks at and throws away, her face scrunched in distaste. I guess when you're beautiful it's hard to have ugly things around you.

My sweet-smelling, scary mother. Once she lightly brushed my shoulder with her icy hand when she strode past me, and my whole body arched towards her. Was it possible, in her fierce, proud, detached way, she loved us?

7
KIDNAP

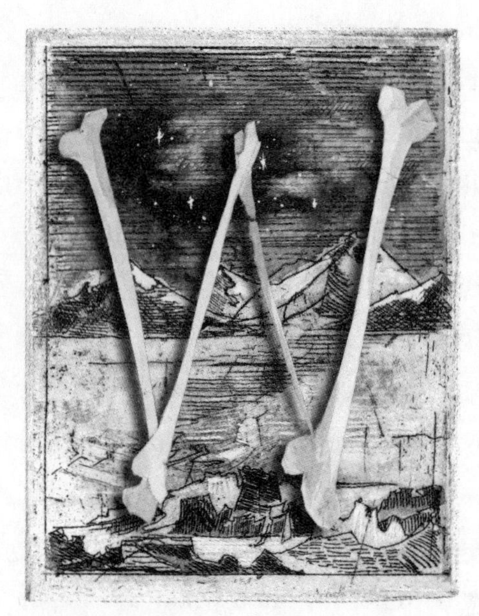

E WERE ASLEEP WHEN the gods came. Jor and Fen curled on their mats in the corners, snorting and spluttering, me stretched out on one bench, Mum on another. It happened so fast even Fen didn't have time to bite or Jor to spit poison when gods blasted into our cave and seized us.

I heard Mum screaming. I jerked awake and then

someone grabbed me. I saw them bind and gag her, squirming and wriggling, her club useless by her side as I was bundled into a scratchy sack. I punched and shrieked. I heard Fen yowling and Jor hissing. Mum couldn't break free of her bonds. My mother, Angrboda, the distress-bringer, whom I never saw alive again.

A part of me thought, *Mum cares! The gods had to tie her up to grab us*. I'd assumed she'd just hand us over to anyone who asked. In fact, I don't know why they didn't. Bet she'd have said yes, take them, praise the giants, I'm free of the brats.

And then up, upside down, flung over a shoulder and carried out. Thump. Thump. Thump. Stomping, stumbling, jolted from side to side and up and down, like a smoked salmon. Splashing through water again and again. I was soaked. I was dizzy. We were moving so fast, crunching through ice and snow, then twigs snapping and branches whipping past and the smell of mould and leaves and the hooting of owls and snarling of wolves. Our captors moved swiftly, pounding through forests and splashing through lakes.

And all the while I was thinking, *Dad loves us after all. Maybe Mum threw him out for good, and now he's kidnapped us. He couldn't bear the thought of never seeing his children again. A love-snatch.*

What a surprise. What a shock.

'Dad wants us with him in Asgard,' I shouted to my brothers.

'What will I eat?' said Fen.

I don't know why Fen expected me to know the answer.

What would our life be like living with Dad in a gleaming gold palace? I wasn't sure what a palace was. An extra big cave, maybe? I was excited, stunned. Dad loved us so much he'd had us kidnapped.

What other reason could there be?

PART 2
Asgard

8

THE SKY FORTRESS

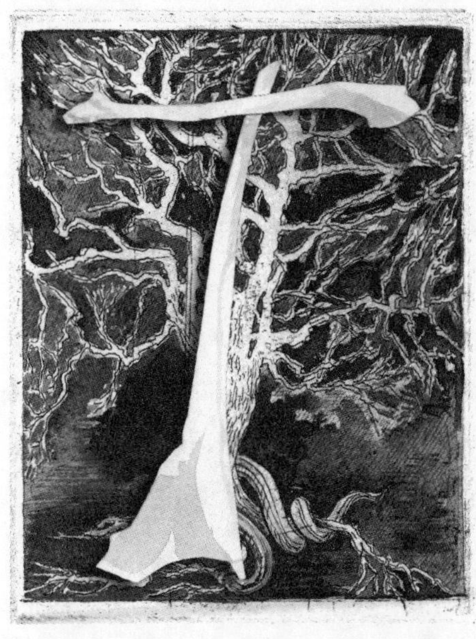

HE LIGHT BLINDED me as the sack was yanked off. I blinked, my eyes smarting, my head spinning. My body ached and my throat was parched. Everywhere I looked I saw gleam and glitter, half-built luminous halls studded with silver and gold. It was too bright. Above us the billowing blue sky enfolded me like a soft cloak, and Yggdrasil, the World Tree that holds the heavens, branched out above me. Asgard, sky fortress of the gods, green and golden, with breezes and eternal sunshine. The air was sweet, perfumed, and my nostrils twitched. The smell was cloying, like too much honey swallowed at once. There was no snow, no ice, no pelting rain and gnawing winds. I raised my face to the sky and felt my skin tingling in the warmth.

The lush plains and meadows stretched out further than I could see in all directions, the gilded palaces, the flaming rainbow bridge arching into the sky. Towering walls encircled the gods' glowing citadel. I'd always thought Dad was lying when he boasted about Asgard's golden halls. In fact, he had not even begun to describe its wonders. I thought of our raven-dark world, our glacier mountains, our belching volcanoes and ironwoods.

I didn't think about my mother.

There was a buzz of talk, murmurings. I focused my eyes, shielding them from the glare. I thought we'd be taken to Dad's palace. But we weren't. We were beside a rippling pool of blue-black water. If I cared about such things, I might have thought it was beautiful.

We'd been dumped in the middle of a circle of newly carved, ivory-white thrones, one High Seat much larger and greater than the others. The gathering gods wore soft clothes in purples and mauves and blues. I felt hot and ugly in my long bearskin, like an animal. I was dazzled by so much colour, so much light. I couldn't believe where I was, a guest of these glittering beings who stalked about like a herd of shining beasts.

Jor was still thrashing and hissing in his sack, venom dribbling. Fen was rolling in the grass, waving his paws. I was sitting, huddled, hiding my legs.

I didn't understand what was happening. *The gods have strange ideas of hospitality*, I thought. *Since when do you bundle visitors into sacks, then drop them on their heads like carcasses instead of leading them to a place of honour, offering warm water, towels, food and drink?*

All around me, the gods took their seats. I recognised

some. Who wouldn't know Thor, red-bearded, built like a volcano, swinging his hammer over his shoulder and glaring at us from his throne? And a beautiful goddess with tumbling hair like spun flax, holding her nose, eyes as bright as dragon fire, fiddling with the necklace of twisted gold that gleamed on her white neck. That was Freyja. And another, Idunn, the keeper of the gods' immortal youth, clutching her basket of golden apples, pressing a cloth to her face as she gagged at my stench.

The one I didn't see anywhere in the throng was Loki, father of lies, father of us. I was surprised – he'd gone to so much trouble to snatch us, you'd think the least he would do is show up. Had he already changed his mind?

Children, some older, some younger than me, hid behind their parents' thrones, the bolder ones peeking out to point. Others approached Fen, daring to get too close till their parents yanked them back.

Why did Loki's children merit such a gathering?

Little Hnoss, Freyja's radiant, honeyed girl, pretty face, pretty feet, pretty everything that I am not, screamed when she saw us. Hnoss, with her nose in the air. 'What's it doing here?' she screeched, till Freyja jerked her eyes at her husband, who snatched the squalling brat up in his arms and carried her off, wailing.

'It stinks!' she shrieked. 'Make it go away.'

It's not my fault I smell, you sow's daughter. I was born like this.

I want to curl up, hide, vanish.

Jor thrashed and writhed in his sack, tearing at the hemp with his fangs, spitting poison. The seated gods shuddered. A few of the children screamed.

I glanced at Fen. He was shaking himself out, pretending to be a playful cub. Fenrir was more vicious than Jor – he just looked more cuddly.

'Loki's monsters,' I heard someone mutter. They scowled at us, stiff with dislike. You'd think we'd gatecrashed a party instead of being dragged here in a bag.

I reminded myself I was an immortal goddess, as much as them.

I looked around the assembled gods once more. Could Loki be hiding, waiting to leap out and yell, 'Boo!!'? Because Dad loved practical jokes. Did you know he once sneaked into Thor's wife's bedroom, lopped off her rippling gold hair while she snored and left her bald? I remembered him telling Mum about it and both of them hooting with laughter.

Ha ha. Not.

Deformity fails to amuse me. Actually, to be fair, nothing amuses me. But I digress.

Nope, no Dad. And then it occurred to me that perhaps he had nothing to do with bringing us here.

I'd be lying if I said I wasn't afraid.

Were we being *judged* at a gods' council? But judged for what?

The assembled gods fell silent as an immortal, bristling with majesty, strode into the circle of thrones. He wore a broad-brimmed blue hat, his boiling single eye fixed on us. I knew this must be Odin, the One-Eyed King of the Gods, Dad's blood brother. The

Wizard King, Spear God, Battle Wolf, Lord of Poetry (gag), Father of Magic, King of the Slain. Two ravens perched on his shoulders; two huge wolves skulked by his sides. Power poured from him. I had never felt so crippled, so small. I struggled to stand but I was shaking too much.

His wolves bristled at Fen, and Fen snarled back, fur prickling, hackles rising. One-Eye whispered to his pair, and they sank to the ground.

Fen strutted off, baying his victory, then sat back on his haunches, lifted his leg and started licking his rear.

The gods roared with laughter. Even I almost smiled.

One-Eye walked towards the sack containing the squirming Jor and without a word grabbed him by the tail and hurled him high into the sky over Asgard's walls.

I still remember that moment. Jor's looping body, his maddened hissing shrieks as he tumbled and vanished. It was so fast it took me a moment to realise what had happened.

My snake brother Jor was gone.

Good riddance.

9
JUDGEMENT

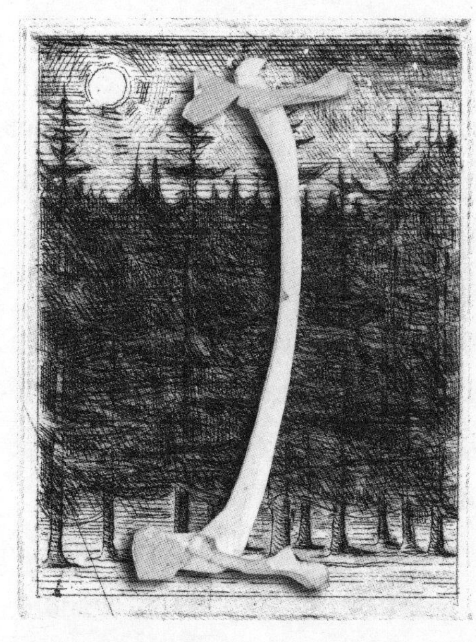

FELT A FLICKER OF pure joy.

'He is fated to harm us so I've hurled him into the sea,' announced One-Eye.

'What sea?' I whispered. As if I were planning a visit to the ocean depths one day. I guess I was in shock.

I could feel the gods suck in their breath. I didn't know the rules. You don't ask a king questions – you answer them. Remember that when you find yourself in front of me.

'He will grow large enough to circle the world and bite his own tail in the ocean surrounding Midgard. The snake was a threat to us all,' said One-Eye. I felt him boring into me, reading my thoughts. I shrank, waiting for the blow to fall.

'The other two will be kept here.'

The gods muttered, shook their heads, scowled. But One-Eye is their chieftain, what he says, goes. He rose and left, his blue cloak sweeping behind him.

I'm safe. I'm safe.

Shaking and swaying, I tried to stay upright, then sank into the soft grass. Jor's fate wasn't mine. My body ached and my legs trembled. I felt as gnarled as a troll. I realised I'd been holding my breath.

So. One hateful, frightening brother gone. A shadow crossed my mind, which I brushed off. Who wouldn't dispose of Jor, given the chance? But I couldn't get the image out of my head, Jormungand tumbling out of Asgard, flailing and falling and spitting and smashing smack into the salt sea and then sinking down to the bottom. I imagined him growing and growing, circling the world, squeezing Midgard beneath the waters.

We'll be safer without him, I thought. *It had to be done.*

You always think the hammer is going to hit someone else.

I stayed sitting by the sun-dappled pool, uncertain of what to do, where to go, watching the glimmering goddesses walking lightly on Asgard's springy sweet earth. I felt like dung on their dainty shoes.

The Asgard children, a gaggle of young immortals, came out from behind their parents' thrones to gawp.

We eyed each other.

I'd never met strangers before. I felt shy, uneasy. I was a goddess, same as them, but they'd been born here, and I was born in Jotunheim. Would they think me more giant than god and shun me? (I really hate children. They're cruel, and they mock. I hate grown-ups too, of course. Actually, don't get me started: I hate everyone.)

Fen shook himself and bounded off into the meadow

grass of the splendid plain surrounding us. Most of the brats ran after him, shouting. Fenrir rolled on the ground. Washed his face with his paws. Played dead.

I watched Thor's red-faced sons throw a branch for him, laughing when he jumped up, snatched it in his fierce jaws and snapped it in two. I'd seen him do this many times, play with a dog or wolf and then suddenly bite its head off. He should have been a storm god, raging and pillaging, just for the pleasure of destroying. He'd have loved that.

One-Eye's thuggish-looking boy, Vidar, approached him. He wore the strangest shoe, thick with leather scraps bound on a sole of iron. In all my time with the gods I never heard him speak. Probably because the little toad thought I wasn't worth speaking to. Vidar whistled at Fen. The wolf hesitated, trotted a few steps towards him, then stopped, his grey fur bristling, his tail rigid, then retreated, snarling. Vidar burst into tears and his mother whisked him away.

Thor's beefy daughter Thrud, with sticky-out teeth like tumbled rocks, looked at me, recoiled, and ran to join her brothers chasing Fen in the meadow.

I just wanted everyone to go away and leave me alone, but two boys remained. They whispered and pointed. I pulled my bearskin robe around me, despite the heat, trying to hide my legs. I heard the names they called me behind their hands. Cripple girl. Rotten herring. Death daughter.

They crept closer, and their mother turned and gave me a look of hate.

'Keep away from that monster,' Sigyn hissed, shooing her boys from me. That's how I met my half-brothers for the first time. I didn't know Dad had other children in Asgard. I didn't even know he had a wife. I just stood there, shaking, my mouth gaping. Dad's other family. The ones he can dress up and show the world. We embarrassed him. We shamed him. *That's why he isn't here*. We're like the uncouth country cousins breaking into the great hall expecting a rousing gift-filled welcome and then stopping short as no high table seat is offered and our kin won't acknowledge us.

I don't think they needed to be told to keep away

from me. I'd never been the most popular girl at the feast. In fact, I'm not usually *at* the feast. Somehow the messenger never arrives to invite me.

Now it's just me, and a single god, Hod. Everyone else has fled.

I stumble over to him. He's blind, oblivious that he's alone.

'Where's Loki?' I ask.

'Loki has business with the mason building our walls,' said the blind one, crinkling his nose, looking in the wrong direction.

'Will he be back soon?'

Hod shrugs. 'Loki comes and goes.'

How awful to be blind, I think.

Then someone shouts at me:

'Leave this sacred place. Council is over. What are you waiting around for?'

It is Heimdall, watchman of the gods. His gold teeth flash as he orders us away. I wonder if one day a dwarf will come and tear out his teeth, to fashion into bracelets.

IO

I ALLOW MYSELF TO DREAM

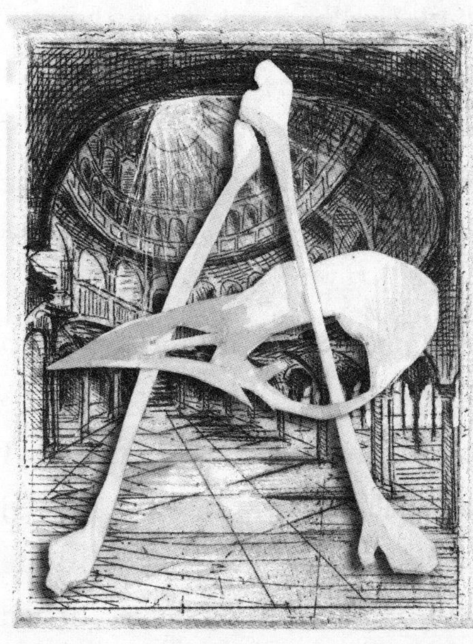

SGARD WAS A building site. Everywhere I roamed I heard hammering and pounding, saw walls rising, masons shouting and roofs being thatched with silver and gold. The vast half-built palaces cascaded into the distance, glowing in the sunshine. My storm-home was bleak and dim, blue-cold. Here, all was brilliance and warmth, golden pillars and shining roofs. This was the beginning of eternity, the start of the gods' reign. They'd conquered the giants and established their dominion over the nine worlds. Now they were building their heavenly stronghold and I was joining them.

'Go on, give us a smile,' yelled a spike-nosed builder, standing high on a roof.

'Why so grim?' another giant shouts down at me.

There's nothing that makes a girl feel less like smiling than some oaf leering at her to change her face. My face isn't the problem.

I ignored them and lumbered past, hoping they'd fall to their deaths.

Everything here was so much taller, brighter, better. I wondered if any of these palaces would be mine. I hoped I wouldn't have to share with Fen and Dad. If I were allowed to build a hall of my own, I'd already found the perfect spot: by a stream, in the shade. I smell like a corpse whenever the sun leaves her tomb. I prefer it when the moon leaves his grave mound to circle the sky.

Vast, sweltering Asgard was my home now, and I would try to belong. I allowed myself to dream.

I wandered like an exultant ghost. I still could not believe I would be living in this gilded kingdom. Only one palace was complete, Gladsheim, where the gods and goddesses had their thrones. I peeked inside. Everything in the great council chamber was made of gold.

I watched some children squealing as they played with a rolled-up bearskin outside Gladsheim. They threw it back and forth amongst four, while a fifth tried to grab the hide. Then they saw me, dropped the bearskin and ran away.

Nothing I wasn't used to. I heard the roarings of a river, thought I would cool my putrid legs in it. But as I headed for the water a gargantuan hall loomed up, far bigger than any I'd passed. In front of it stood the most beautiful tree I'd ever seen, glistening with gold foliage.

But what caught my eye were the hundreds of gigantic doorways being carved into the walls.

I peered in. You could march 250 trolls standing side by side through each one, easily (well, that is if you could get trolls to march, which is unlikely, but you get the picture).

Gleaming swords, heavy, carved, lit the hall. Rainbows of light bounced off the blades. The rafters were made of spear shafts and thatched with overlapping golden shields.

Row after row of empty benches stretched into the distance. So many tables, so many shields and axes and lances and swords, glowing red-gold mail coats, helmets too many to count.

'What is this place?' I asked one of the masons, hewing and lashing bright shields to the roof.

'This is where Odin's chosen warriors will come, to feast and drink and fight,' he replied, wiping sweat off his brow.

I didn't know what a warrior was. A new race of gods, perhaps? But I didn't want to show my stupidity and ignorance. Even the dullest-witted builder knew things

I did not. (I'd been shut away in a cave. I knew nothing.)

'Why?' I asked. 'Who will they be fighting?'

The mason shrugged. 'I don't ask questions – I just do what I'm told, take the gold and get out.'

No one stopped me entering.

I curled up on one of the long wooden benches and I slept.

II

BALDR, MY BALDR

HEARD A HISS and immediately woke. I feared for a moment my snake brother had returned. Mercifully, not. There were winged women lurking in the shadows. Big, ugly, broad-faced harridans wearing helmets and chain mail. One polished the rows of curved drinking horns, snug in their holders. Others sat at a loom made of weapons and entrails and skulls. I sniffed the rich smell of roasting boar, and bubbling honeyed mead in a gigantic vat.

'What are you doing? Get out. You don't belong here,' screamed one, and her voice was like a raven's venomous cackle. 'This is the feast hall of dead warriors. We Valkyries choose who comes here, and we most certainly don't choose you.'

She glared at me with bloodshot eyes. I have a good sense of smell, and I smelled death on these women. The benches were waiting for the battle-dead.

'Brynhild, she's nothing, leave her,' said another.

'I'm a goddess,' I said. 'Daughter of Loki. And you're what? Servants? Barmaids?'

The woman spat and glared at me with her narrow red eyes. 'We are shield-maidens. We decide who lives and who dies in battle. We are the choosers of the slain.'

'No wonder you smell, Carrion Girl,' I said. Yeah I know, pot calling the kettle black, blah blah blah.

'We will bring the bravest here to Valhall, the hall of

the slain, to fight for the gods in the Last Battle at the End of Days, when the forces of chaos overrun Asgard,' said another.

I went rigid. The Last Battle? *What* Last Battle? Who are the forces of chaos? Why was there always so much I didn't know? We were at the beginning of eternity, and already time was collapsing towards an ending.

One-Eye entered, his wolves padding beside him. I recoiled but I'd been seen. Of course I'd been seen – the Great Wizard sees everything.

Had I done something wrong sheltering in Valhall? You can never tell what One-Eye is thinking. But Dad and he were blood-brothers. Surely he'd never hurt me.

'She can sleep here,' said One-Eye. 'Until I find a better home for her.'

The crones muttered and spat.

'Thank you,' I said. I was afraid he'd change his mind, so I backed out of the nearest door, stumbling. And collided with someone.

I felt arms grab me, steadying me. I regained my

balance, turned, gabbling thanks, and I saw him.

His eyes were blue like glaciers. I'd never seen eyes like that. Golden light blazed from him.

I felt the air prickling against my skin. My hands reached up to hide my flushed cheeks.

He looked at me and smiled. Baldr, most beautiful, most glorious, wisest and kindest of the gods.

'Hello, Hel,' he said.

He knows my name. I was speechless.

I see it in my mind, again and again. I hear how he said my name, like it was just a name, like I was just a goddess, not a filthy walking corpse.

And then he picks me up and whirls me around until I am laughing and dizzy and he is laughing.

I feel like I am flying. My robe swirls around me. No one has ever picked me up. No one has ever touched me.

I cling to him. He smells of blackberries and apples and scythed grass. I grip his white arms. I have never felt so light. I have never felt like a creature of air before.

He sets me down and I fall over.

My cursed legs.

'Sorry, sorry,' he says, grabbing my hands and pulling me to my feet. His hands are warm. I'm trembling. And I think, *He forgot about my twisted legs. That's why he plopped me down.*

'Are you all right?'

I nod.

He beams at me. His smile is a tiny bit crooked. I have never seen anything or anyone so lovely.

'My son loves being whirled about,' he says.

I am panting. Slowly catching my breath. The world is swimming and shimmering about me. I hear his words and I don't.

He has a son. Does that mean he also has . . .

'Where is he?' I ask.

Baldr smiles. 'Forseti is with Nanna.'

'Nanna?'

'His mother. My wife.'

I'm good at hiding my feelings. My face is still. I bend down to straighten my skirts, covering my trembling legs.

His wife. Of course he has a wife.

I look at Baldr, the sun haloing him with light, smiling at me (smiling!) and I know. He sees past my deformity: he doesn't see a monster, he sees a girl. He tells me that my hair is beautiful, that it looks like shooting stars. I have a feeling inside me as if ice is crackling. I take a deep breath, hoping to breathe him in, keep some bit of him with me. The most beautiful of the gods, the most beautiful creature I have ever seen, ever, even in my dreams, is there, in front of me, not screaming, not trying to run, not recoiling in horror. But smiling.

And then his smile broadens, deepens. I want this to last forever.

Then I see. He isn't smiling at me. He's smiling at someone behind me.

His son I hope. Fathers smile at their children. (They do, don't they? I never know for sure about such things.)

I am frightened to turn round. Because so long as I don't I can still hold the hope in my heart that Baldr's smile is for me.

'Nanna,' he says.

I try to look as if my heart hasn't cracked. I watch as he goes up to her, and wraps his arms round her, nuzzling his face into her hair and whispering something. She smiles.

Vicious feelings erupt in me. I hate Nanna. I hate her nervous sideways glance, her stupid whiny itty-bitty voice, the way her rat-brown hair oozes from her scalp, her pink pig ears, the way she constantly touches him, every gesture flaunting *he's mine, mine, not yours, mine.*

I don't despair.

Maybe if he gets to know me, I think.

Maybe . . .

12

HE LIKES ME, I KNOW HE DOES

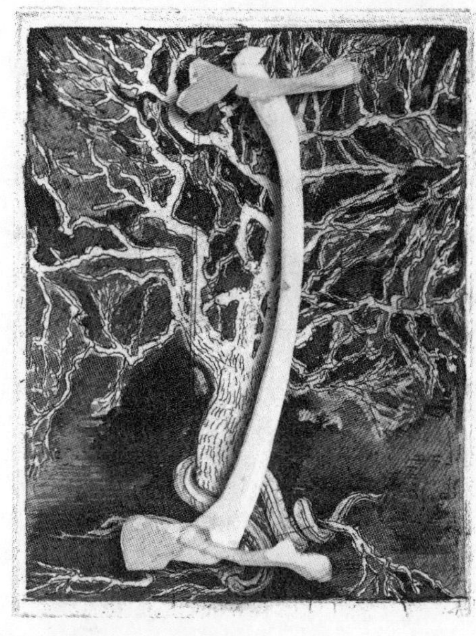

FOLLOW HIM. Quietly.

Day after day I creep out of Valhall, watch where Baldr goes, and contrive a reason to be there.

Baldr's shadow, the gods call me. What do I care? Because he likes me. I know he does.

He talks to me about the gods, asks me questions, tells me things. He makes me laugh. Laughter feels strange in my throat. When I'm with him, I forget I'm a monster. (He says that maybe the healing goddess Eir could help my legs. I'm filled with hope, but of course she can't. If I'd been ALL dead that would have been a different matter. Just my bad luck, as always.)

'Well, Hel,' he said.

(It rhymes! He made my name rhyme.) His hair is white gold, his brow smooth and fair. He is One-Eye's son. I don't hold that against him. After all, we don't choose our parents, any more than they choose their children.

'There's something you need to know.'

13

ONE DAY HE'D BE MINE

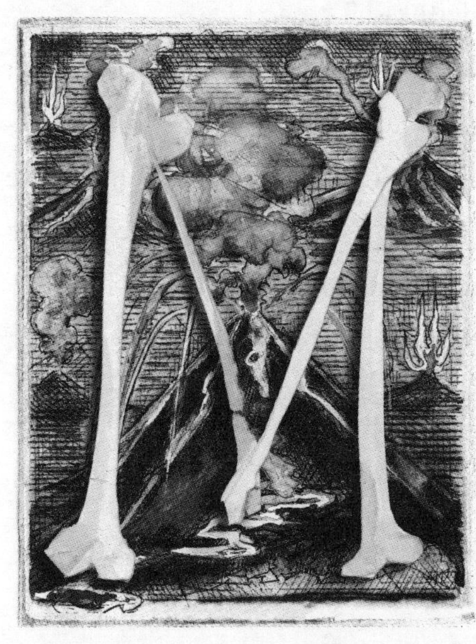

Y HEART POUNDED. *He's going to tell me he loves me.*

'Do you know what is prophesied about Fenrir?' said Baldr.

I hid my disappointment. My face was still. *He's not ready yet. I understand. Of course I understand.*

'What prophesy about Fen?' I said. 'That he rids the world of rats?'

'That he will kill Odin at the End of Days,' whispered Baldr. 'During the Last Battle at Ragnarok.'

I know that Fen is vicious, but how could he ever be powerful enough to kill the Wizard King?

'Fen?'

'And Jormungand will kill Thor.'

That I could believe.

'Who foretold this?'

'The Fates,' said Baldr. 'That's why you were all kidnapped.'

My throat tightened. Did I *want* to know my future?

Of course I did. Who could resist? I know, I know, a man's fate should be safely hidden from him, but I am bolder.

'What about me?' Maybe, just maybe, they'd said that Baldr and I . . .

'Nothing.'

For a moment, I was insulted.

'So I don't kill anyone?'

'Not that they mentioned.'

I nodded. What could I say? I wasn't exactly the axe-wielding type. Anyone could outrun me.

And then I thought, *Am I so unworthy the Fates have* nothing *to say about me? Just my hateful brothers?*

On the other hand, that meant Fenrir was in danger, and I wasn't.

Did I care that my remaining brother needed to beware? Are you joking? I was delighted at the thought of being an only child.

I smiled up at Baldr. He alone of the gods had been kind to me.

His voice was like honeyed mead, dripping into my mouth.

He had a wife. He had a son.

I didn't care.

One day he'd be mine.

14
CRÈCHE OF HORRORS

T HAD TO HAPPEN. One day Dad returned, leading a colt with eight legs. My trickster father, Loki. The sly one. The giant's son. My bad blood.

I watched as he swaggered through Asgard, teasing and laughing, slapping gods on the back. Whispering jokes and gulping mead. Boasting about how he'd enticed the wall-builder's stallion away by changing himself into a mare. (As if you'd want to *brag* about that.)

'And now, thanks to me,' he gloated, 'we saved Freyja, the sun and the moon, and got our Asgard wall built for free! That disgusting giant couldn't build the ramparts in six months without his stallion to help so he lost the bargain as well as his head.'

So the lazy, two-faced gods cheated a poor giant out of his promised reward. Oath-breakers.

What a surprise. Not.

'That's a fine horse,' said One-Eye.

'He's yours,' said Loki. 'He's my son, Sleipnir, and the greatest horse alive. He can outrun anything, and take you anywhere you want to go, even to the land of the dead and back.'

I listened, horrified, as Dad shamelessly added a HORSE to his menagerie. What next? A boar?

But One-Eye smiled and nodded. The colt trotted over to him.

Then Dad saw me. His face went grey, as grey as Sleipnir.

'What is IT doing here?'

One-Eye put his arm around Dad and murmured in his ear. They walked off together into One-Eye's gleaming hall.

Thanks, Dad. Great to see you too.

Let's pause and take a closer look at just some of Dad's children.

Eight legs (Sleipnir)
Four legs (Fenrir)
No legs (Jormungand)
Corpse legs (yours truly)

I'm getting a leggy theme here. What's next in the progeny department, Dad – a centipede?

What lovely siblings I have. My new half-brother is an eight-legged horse that Dad gave birth to while he was prancing around as a mare. (His saga gets worse and worse, doesn't it?) Then my full bad-blood brothers: a wolf and a snake. Then assorted man-eating hags.

(I never asked him about the ogresses. I guess I didn't really want to know the answer. Would you?) Dad and all his hideous brats, popping up everywhere. What was he trying to do, create his own crèche of horrors?

He got away with everything, my flickering, deceitful, shape-shifting father. Sometimes he was a handsome god. Sometimes an old woman. Sometimes a mare, or a salmon, or a fly.

That's Loki, turning a disaster into a triumph.

Shame he could never work the same miracle on me.

I used to pretend I could shape-shift like my father. I'd look at my half-dead body, close my eyes and imagine myself transformed into a whole living one. Not even anything special, just legs that were ivory-pink instead of festering, gangrenous black.

So why didn't the gods just kill us, Loki's monstrous children? Stupid question.

We were related to the gods, the children of a god. You don't pollute a place like Asgard with gods' spilled blood. Even bad blood.

Bet they wished they could. Bet they wished they had. But you can't change your fate. You can only try to hide from it.

For a while the gods thought they could tame Fen. Maybe they hoped Asgard's balmy air would sweeten his breath and ease his rage. Ha. I could have told them that was a non-starter. Especially as he got bigger and bigger, less and less playful.

Instead, they came up with subtler plans.

15

DEATH TUMBLE

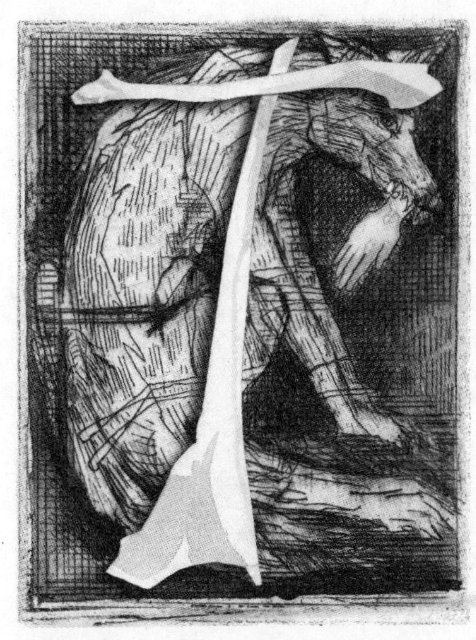

HE GODS GATHERED in one of their glorious meadows and whistled for Fen. I saw Tyr and Heimdall lugging a massive, iron-linked chain between them. It clumped and thudded, each fetter broad as an oak trunk. I remember the breeze, warm on my skin and the smell of apple blossom.

Fen sidled up.

'Wolf,' said Tyr. 'Are you eager for fame?'

Fen said nothing, watching them with his burning yellow eyes.

'Are you as strong as this chain? I've bet you are – Heimdall insists that you're not.'

Fen sniffed the chain then sat back on his haunches. *He's got bigger*, I thought. *A lot bigger*. His mighty paws no longer looked too large for his body.

'If you can break it, you'll be renowned for your strength throughout the nine worlds.'

I watched Fen eye up the fetters. The gods gathered round, eager for the sport. Magni, Thor's son, tried to push one of the links, and gave up.

Suddenly Fen bared his terrible teeth.

'Bind me,' he said.

Fen let the gods wind the heavy fetters round his neck, his legs and his hairy belly till he was trussed like a ham. I could feel Fen playing with them as he sank beneath the chain's weight. I knew he was pretending; I don't think the gods did.

‘Ready?’ they asked.

Fenrir flexed his muscles. The chain shuddered, but didn’t crack.

The gods held their breath.

Fenrir lashed against it, straining his muscles, bracing his heavy paws. Then suddenly the chain exploded, every link shattering, flying through the air like rocks. The gods leaped back. Magni shrieked and burst into tears as a link gashed his shoulder. His father slapped his face.

The next day, they tried again. This time with a chain twice as strong as the first, a chain with links so huge that even Thor struggled to lift them.

Again Fenrir, eager for fame, and keen to mock, let the gods bind him.

There was a clinking and clanking as my brother heaved and strained. This time I knew he wasn’t pretending. He dug his paws into the ground, filled his chest with air, straining and growling and flexing every muscle in his body. Then – TWANG! – the bonds burst, the links breaking into a thousand pieces.

The next time they tried it was with a fetter as soft and smooth as a silken ribbon, but woven by dwarves with cunning and magic, from the sound of a cat walking and a woman's beard, the roots of a rock, the sinews of a bear, the breath of a fish, the spit of a bird. Deep dwarf magic, infecting chains with what is invisible and unheard. Fen of course was suspicious, but he craved glory and renown. (Let his fate be a lesson to all fame-seekers.)

'You're sure to be able to break it,' said Tyr. 'And, if you can't, we'll free you.'

(We all know how much a god's oath is worth. Stupid, proud Fen.)

Fen agreed. 'On one condition,' he snarled. 'That one of you place his right hand in my mouth.' Actually, he should have insisted one of them stuff their head in his maw.

The gods shifted nervously. I certainly wasn't volunteering. I wanted nothing to do with the gods and their games. Dad also kept quiet.

Tyr looked round at the cowardly gods. All avoided

his eyes. Then he stepped forward and slowly put his right hand in Fen's mouth. Fen I knew wanted to bite it off immediately, just for fun. The others wound the ribbon tightly round Fen's neck and legs and body.

I couldn't breathe. I prayed to the ancestors that Fen would be bound and I'd be rid of him.

'Go on, Wolf, break free!' urged the gods.

But the more Fen strained, the tighter the ribbon imprisoned his body. He twisted and grunted and fought, but he was caught.

'Free me,' growled Fen, panting.

The gods laughed instead, whooping and rejoicing at his binding.

All except Tyr, who screamed when Fen bit off his hand and swallowed it.

Then Fen threw back his head and howled. He bared his steel-sharp teeth and thrashed and roared his eternal vengeance. Fires burned from his eyes and nostrils. He looked nothing like a cub any more. He looked like a wolf of Ironwood.

The gods recoiled. I also lurched back, and that's when Odin seized me by my hair and hurled me high into the sky over Asgard's high walls.

Dad did nothing to save me. His mouth was full of air.

'Hel!' bellowed One-Eye. I heard his voice as I somersaulted through the clouds, the citadel of Asgard shrinking in the distance. My death tumble. My skyfall.

His voice was like the crashing of the ocean onto jagged rocks. 'You will rule the worlds below the world. You will provide drink and lodging to all those sent to you, host everyone who dies of sickness or old age. They are your people – you are their queen. Go and rule Niflheim.'

What was this fearsome decree?

Day slowly turned to night, and still I tumbled through the air, a shrieking, screaming speck falling through the universe into a geyser of light plumes rising into the darkness. Billowing blood-red, seaweed-green and sun-orange lights poured up like a roaring curtain as I tore through the swirling spirals of colour. The sky was studded with stars.

I heard a wolf howl and then I crashed through the worlds into the void of eternal darkness. Icy frost reached for me, and I fell into its shrouded embrace.

PART 3
Niflheim

16

QUEEN OF THE DEAD

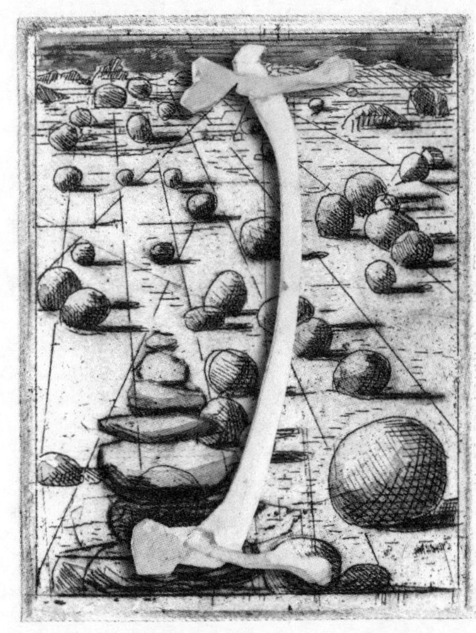

TUMBLED INTO THE dark and huddled within its folds. Murky black. Mist. Ice. The stink of sulphur. Did I lie stunned and shocked on the clammy rocks for hours, nights, weeks, years? Who knows? Time means nothing to me. I fell out of time long ago.

I'd always been lost between worlds and never more

than now. Half alive. Half dead. Half goddess. Half giant. And now I was trapped in Niflheim, the ancient fog world beneath the worlds. A living queen presiding over the dead: that was One-Eye's cruel decree. I howled like a wolf pack, screaming at my bad fate, hurling curses at One-Eye and the merciless gods until my throat was parched and all I could do was choke and rasp. Remember, I was only a child. I was no more than fourteen winters old. They entombed a living child in a gigantic grave mound. I didn't think about Jor trapped beneath the waves, or Fen raging in his fetters, chained to a boulder deep underground. All of us monstrous children, each in our own prison, waiting for the doom of the gods and our deadly revenge.

If I am in a charitable mood – which is rare, but when I am I think, *If I knew that someone or something was out to kill me, I'd do whatever I had to do to stop them.*'

So, fair enough, do what you want with my evil brothers. But I wasn't out to kill anyone. The Fates said nothing about *me*. There was no prophesy. No threat. **SO WHY WAS I THROWN DOWN HERE?** What danger did I pose?

None.

Yet the gods feared me. The great gods, so scared of a crippled girl that they had to exile her below the worlds.

One-Eye had clearly said Niflheim. That I'd reign over the dead. Just what I'd always wanted, to rule the fateless. I mean, who wouldn't long to spend their eternal life hanging out with corpses in a land of perpetual winter's night? I'm to be a queen. But of whom? Odin said *people*. What are people? I had never seen or heard of such creatures. Whatever they were, I was ordered to be their host. What did that mean? Provide canapés and nibbles, wheel out a welcome feast? Would I be managing a zoo filled with ghostly beasts and headless trolls?

And then I thought, *Where are all these decomposing guests, anyway?*

I peered through the swirling death mist. I was

surrounded by sheer cliffs and hills of dizzying steepness. Above me, no sky, just the spreading roots of Yggdrasil, the ash tree, whose leafy top branches I'd seen in Asgard. I felt as if I were in some claggy cave, but more dismal than any cave I'd ever known. And so cold. Colder than Ironwood. The icy air stung my throat. It was like breathing knives. I opened my clenched hands, and black sands etched with silver poured from my fists.

All around me burned fires, hissing and spitting in the gloom, strange fires that gave no heat but offered pinpricks of light. The noise was terrible: moaning winds, tumbling rocks, lava spurting high above islands dotting a boiling river studded with ice. I covered my ears while the ancient fog world belched, steam shrieking as it burst from fissures in the rocks into the fetid air. For once, the toxic smell wasn't me.

From somewhere far, far away I heard the rumble of water. A waterfall?

Why hadn't I listened when giants told tales of how

Niflheim existed long before the worlds were created? I knew nothing about it. I'm an immortal goddess – what did I care where mortal things went when they died?

I couldn't take in the full horror of my vicious fate, the wretched outcome of my bad blood. Yet I, guilty of nothing, was banished to this storm-wracked world. I would never see the sun or the moon again. I would never smell anything fresh or sweet. I would never feel warm. I would putrefy here.

I would never see Baldr again.

I sat on the rocks and cried. I only stopped when the far-off howls of a dog joined my shrieks.

I couldn't think. I couldn't move. But the dog sounded unearthly, frightening, a wolf of Ironwood, and I didn't want to be caught in the open like this.

I crept away on my hands and knees through the scouring sleet, feeling my way along the cliffs. I pushed through the blackness, like wading into curtains of squashed flies. Eventually I found a cave and crawled inside. I crouched against the slimy walls and huddled there, bellowing my hate for One-Eye and the gods. The cave – a dank, fumy hole – echoed my wails back to me till I was surrounded by sobs. Stench seeped like silt into every crevasse.

Was this cesspit to be my home? Never. Anywhere had to be better than this despairing place.

And then another thought struck me: maybe I could discover a way out, a way back to the world of the living.

Yes! The dead arrived from somewhere. If I could find that fog road, or that sea on which they sailed, I could go back to the light. Not to my mother who was probably dancing with joy that she was rid of me. Dear old Dad certainly didn't want me. But I'd seek somewhere out of sight so even all-seeing One-Eye wouldn't uncover me. I'm clever, my father's daughter. I know how to hide. I was alive and the land of the dead was no place for me.

One-Eye had banished me to rule here, but his decree didn't say I had to *stay* here, did it? Kings and queens travel. One-Eye was always slipping out of Asgard.

I had to escape.

I shuffled through a deep valley towards the sound of water, sidestepping chasms and bogs. I groped my way through the throttling blackness, trying to breathe despite the choking mist, frost crunching under my feet. I passed sulphur lakes, boiling springs, foaming torrents crackling with ice. The only light came from the occasional spurts of flames. And always precipices, fumes, cold and –

Oh, enough local colour. I'm boring myself. Frankly, if you've seen one sulphurous pit, hideous precipice and poisonous, hissing, foaming river you've seen them all. When it's your turn to travel down the lonely fog road, you can describe its horrors to your heart's content.

I followed the sound of water, as far as I could go. My robes were damp and heavy with sleet. I hoped to find a ship, something that would float me out of this nightmare. The noxious air was growing thick and poisonous. I appeared to be stumbling into a squelching pit. I hesitated, not sure whether to keep going or to retrace my steps.

And then I heard hissing.

I froze.

17
DRAGON

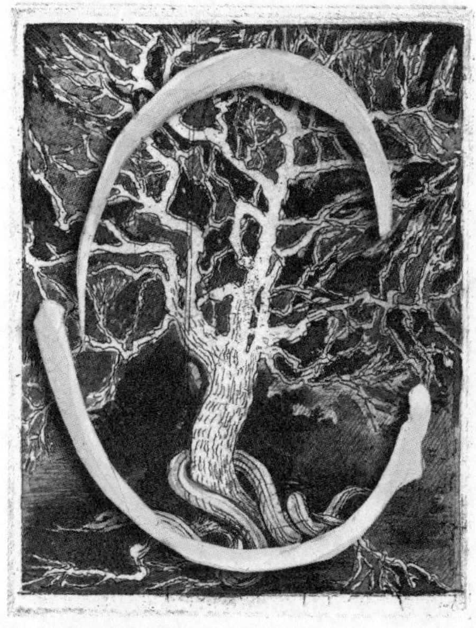

OILED ROUND AN enormous tree root, half in and half out of a seething swamp, was a dragon. It gnawed viciously at the tree roots, which shuddered as if they were alive.

The dragon stopped chewing. He swung his heavy head and opened his mouth, thrashing towards me, splattering me with freezing water.

'Don't you dare touch me!' I screamed. An avalanche of boulders crashed onto his heaving body and sand swirled into his lava eyes.

The dragon stopped. He threw his head wildly about, blinking and shaking. I stood back behind the largest boulder, which had rolled in front of me. I needed to put something, anything, however small, between us.

He sniffed.

'You're a corpse,' he rasped. 'And not a corpse.'

'I'm your queen,' I shrieked. 'Queen of Niflheim. You will die horribly if you touch me.'

The dragon shook his feathered head, his eyes squeezed shut.

'And I am Nidhogg!' bellowed the monster. His breath was venomous and rank. 'I'm sick of gnawing on tree roots. I want real food. I want corpses. Feed me.'

'You'll have your corpses soon enough,' I said.

'Make sure you send them here,' roared the dragon. He curled back around Yggdrasil's roots and savagely bit them.

'Never leave this place,' I ordered.

Nidhogg lowered his gleaming head.

'Keep me fed. I won't budge,' he hissed, blasting me with his poisonous breath.

I crept away from the deepest part of Niflheim, the gruesome sound of the dragon's crunching gradually fading, and headed upwards, feeling my way slowly through the pitch dark. It was a long while before my heart stopped thudding. What other monsters were lying in wait for me in this infernal place?

Another thought struck me. The boulders that had rained on Nidhogg, and the sand that had blinded him. Where had they come from?

But there was no one to answer me.

My feet kept tripping over the slippery rocks as I clawed my way upwards through the gloom out of Nidhogg's venomous valley.

'Get out of my way!' I screamed, stumbling over a rock for the millionth time and falling in the slimy ooze.

The rock immediately rolled off the path into the crevasse below, landing in the churning river with a distant *plock*.

Feeling foolish, and for a moment glad no one was here to witness my idiocy, I ordered a boulder to roll.

It did.

Another to stack itself on top of another.

It did.

I appeared to have power here to command stones.

I made rock after rock smash against the cliffs, screaming and laughing as they splintered and cracked. Shards rained down, splashing into the water below. I punched the air, shrieking, clenching my fists.

I had power. *I* had power. I felt the fiercest joy. I could destroy anyone or anything that threatened me.

And I would. Fate, for once, had smiled on me.

At the bottom of the next valley I came upon the river. It was fast-flowing, filled with chunks of ice, crashing and hurtling against one another. Frost rose from the grey water.

And then I saw I wasn't alone.

18

DEFINITELY DEAD

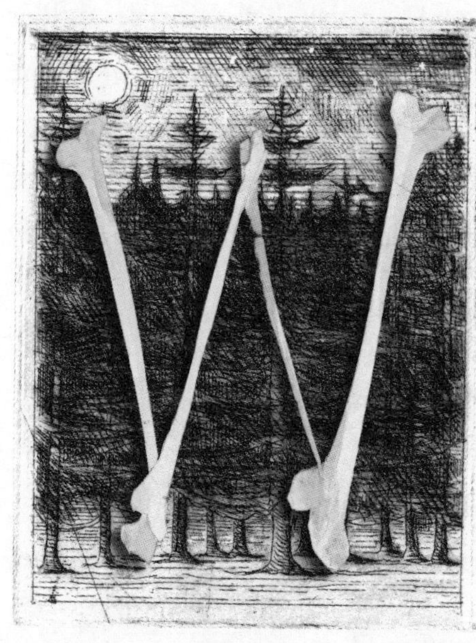

ALKING TOWARDS me through the gloom was a shadow, a sort of shade. I watched, horrified, as she drifted closer, moving soundlessly on bare feet. She was wrapped in skins, but her body was translucent. The reek of death was overpowering.

She was neither troll (head not big enough), nor ogre (not enough heads), nor giant. Nor was she an elf or a dwarf. What kind of creature was she? Whatever she was, she was definitely dead, and definitely coming towards me.

'Stop,' I ordered. 'Don't come any closer.'

Had some baneful fiend sent her to harm me, or to stop me escaping? I'd crush her with a boulder if she took another step. Though, could you kill the dead twice?

The thing obeyed. Enough was left of her face for me to see she was lost and bewildered. And clearly frightened.

She opened her mouth to speak, but no sound came out.

'How did you get here?'

The thing pointed behind her.

'I crossed the Echoing Bridge,' she said faintly. 'After walking down the long fog road for many nights.'

I drank in her words. *Bridge? Road?* Surely if the dead whatever-she-was could walk *down* it, *I* could walk *up* it? After so much searching, I had found an exit.

Holding my nose, I brushed past the cadaver, desperate to find the bridge she spoke of. In the distance I caught a glimpse of gold, and faint shadows billowing and fluttering. Were these dead ... *people*?

I stopped.

'What are you? I asked.

'I was Embla,' said the shade. She was trembling. 'The first woman.'

'What do you mean, the first woman?'

'Where the earth meets the sea,' said Embla in her sing-song voice, 'on the strip of land belonging neither to land nor water, the All-Father Odin and his brothers carved two of us, a man and a woman, from a dead ash and a dead elm tree. They breathed life into us, gave us feelings and heart and wits and sight.'

I listened to the corpse, and I could not believe what I was hearing. My hatred for One-Eye, which I did not think could be greater, rose into my throat like vomit. What a vanity project, to make mortals – people! – just so you could have your own gaggle of worshippers and followers. Wasn't it enough that he had made himself ruler over all the gods? Did he really need to create little creatures out of wood to lord over as well?

The arrogance. The conceit.

So these were the things I was forced to host. One-Eye's driftwood.

'I've died in childbirth, and here I am. Fateless,' said Embla.

My first *guest*. The first of the unwelcome ones I am forced to rule for eternity. Uggh. She looked at me, as if awaiting direction. What was I supposed to do? What I wanted to do was yell, 'Buzz off, Bones! Jump in the river and drown.' But Odin had condemned me to receive anyone who came to me.

Well, I wasn't doing it for nothing. Everyone likes a gift, after all.

'I'm your queen,' I said. 'What have you brought me?'

Embla paused.

'What do you mean?'

I drew myself up as straight as I could.

'You're expecting me to host you in my hall,' I said. 'And not just for a winter, but forever. It is customary to bring gifts to your lord, in thanks for hospitality.'

'What hall?' asked Embla. 'I don't see any hall.'

'This kingdom is my hall,' I said, waving my arms.

'This isn't a hall,' she said.

Wasn't it enough that the dead *stank?* Did they have to be rude as well?

I pointed to the sheer rocks behind me.

'I'm building one over there,' I said.

'When you've *finished* the hall we'll talk about gifts,' said Embla.

'When I've built the hall, you'll be lucky to get the chance to clean it,' I snapped as Embla drifted off. She was a dead piece of driftwood – who was she to argue with me about accommodation? (All right, I know what you're thinking. I really don't have the personality to be an innkeeper. Can I remind you I never asked for this job?)

I could see what was going to happen. It wouldn't just

be one or two or three reeking corpses coming to stay. It would be hundreds. Thousands. Eventually, millions and billions of shades trickling over the bridge, a never-ending malignant ghost stream.

I'd have to build a hall for them. I had no choice.

What then? I'd been ordered to host the dead. *How* do you host people? I'd leave mead as ordered. I just had no intention of wheeling out the hostess trolley and hanging around. Let the dead fend for themselves. Odin made them; let Odin do his own dirty work.

I inched through swirls of fog, my legs aching and numb, as the crash of water grew louder and louder and I saw lights glinting off a golden bridge.

The bridge!

Shining, gleaming, thatched with gold. Sparks of light flashed from its sides and roof. A river thundered below, sullen with blocks of ice, bubbling fumes rising from its torrents. On the other side I could just see a twisting track rising upwards into the gloom, and shadowy forms and corpses coming down it.

I hugged myself for joy. My terrified stumbling around Niflheim had paid off. I'd survived and I'd reached the way out.

Almost beside myself with exhaustion, I willed my collapsing legs and body to carry on. Once across the bridge dividing the land of the living from the land of the dead, I would travel as far as I could. I would find a cave hidden from Odin's baleful eye, deep in Jotunheim. They say he can see anywhere into the nine worlds. Maybe. Could he see me now? I didn't care. I stuck out my tongue.

'That's for you, One-Eye,' I hissed. 'You son of a mare.'

I shuffled to the radiant bridge as fast as I could stagger, closer and closer, my freedom beckoning through the mists, and then stepped onto –

Nothing. I was at the covered bridge's near side, which glowed one pace in front of me, and it was as if I were taking a leap into emptiness. I stepped again, and stayed in my place. I held out my hands – was there some strange force keeping me back? I felt nothing but the chill and choking vapour whirling around me.

I could not put my foot on the bridge. I could not reach out my hand and touch the sides.

'Let me pass!' I ordered. My voice echoed in the valley of death.

Would the bridge obey, as the rocks and boulders had?

I stepped forward, and again did not move. I stretched out my hand and it was blocked. Corpses and spirits wafted silently over the bridge from the other side and passed by me.

All traffic was one way.

And at that moment I knew I was trapped forever. One-Eye had banished me here, and his spells had bound me to this poisonous place as much as any corpse. The dead can never return to the land of the living, and neither could I.

Here I would stay, alive, sealed in a grave barrow until the doom of the gods.

I would never see Baldr again.

I fell to my knees and screamed. I hurled boulders into the river (who knew I had the strength of a troll?), cracking the blocks of ice and splashing the water high into the air. My new-found power astounded me.

Then I collapsed to the frozen earth in tears. I was like a child in a playpen, hurling rocks out. When all the rocks were gone, I was still in prison. Immortal or not, I would sicken and die on this pestilent ground. I heard the dog howling again.

'How did you sneak past me?' came a stern voice. Long-nailed fingers poked my shoulder.

I jerked away.

'Don't touch me!' I whispered.

What ghoulish creature was going to attack now? Let them eat me. I was past caring.

19

GREEN LIKE GANGRENE, BLUE LIKE BRUISES

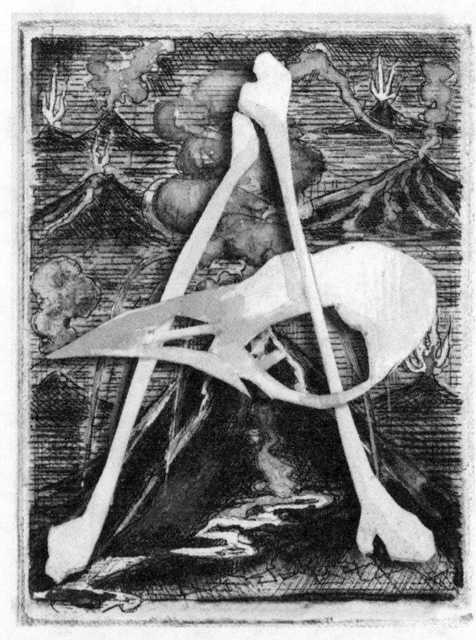

PALE GIANTESS, somewhere between child and mid-grown, peered down at me.

'Why are you crying?' she asked.

I was not expecting this. I definitely was not expecting this. What was a giantess doing in Niflheim?

'Go away,' I said. 'Leave me alone.'

She did not move.

I sneaked a peek at her.

The giantess stood taller than me, but not by much. She looked about my age. But most difficult to take in was that she –

'Are you dead?' I asked.

'Do I look dead?' said the girl.

She looked very alive to me. Positively blooming with health, if you ignored her chalk-white skin, like bleached bones the ravens have pecked dry. Was she a guard One-Eye had set over me? She didn't appear to have any weapons, but she might have spells.

'Are you lost?' I asked. Our breath mingled in the murky air.

The girl snorted.

'I don't think anyone wanders down here by accident.' She looked at me curiously.

'You're not dead, are you?' she said.

'Half,' I said.

'You can't be half,' said the girl. 'It's either/or.'

I shrugged, flicked aside my robes and showed her my

gangrenous legs. She didn't even flinch. Or wrinkle her nose. That was a first.

'I've seen a lot worse,' she said. 'You wouldn't believe the state of some of those fateless ones when they arrive. Who were – I mean, who are you?' She grinned. 'That's not a question I've ever asked before.'

'I'm queen. I'm supposed to rule here,' I said. 'By Odin's decree.'

'Oh,' said the maiden. 'Congratulations?'

We looked at one another and for some reason we both started to laugh. (I don't remember laughing since. What do I have to laugh about?) The sound echoed across the murky valley, bouncing back to us from the cliffs and over the roar of the river.

'I'm Hel,' I said. 'Queen of the Dead.' The words sounded unreal in my mouth.

'I'm Modgud,' said the giantess.

Modgud means *war frenzy*. She was a giantess all right. Like I said, who else gives their children such horrible names? She looked about as frenzied as a nut.

'Did the gods throw you down here too?'

'I don't know any gods,' she said. 'Except Blood Mother – I've heard of her. I guard the bridge.'

Guard? That meant she had power. That meant . . .

I proceeded carefully.

'Why?' I asked.

'To keep out the living,' said Modgud. 'Only the dead can cross the River Gjoll. I'm the warden of the bridge. I protect the boundary between the living and the dead.'

What, she expected an invasion of the living to force their way to the Realm of the Dead before their time? Was she mad?

'Why would anyone alive come *here*?' I asked.

'Seeking wisdom,' said Modgud. 'Hoping for answers. Trying to learn the secrets only the dead know.'

More fool them spying and prying.

I pulled myself to my feet.

'Let me cross.' My voice shook.

Modgud stared at me.

'No,' she said.

'Let me leave,' I said. 'Please.' (The word *please* stuck in my proud throat, but I had to say it.)

'Everyone wants to leave,' said Modgud. 'But you can't.'

'I order you.'

'Order away,' said Modgud. 'Nothing can change.'

'I'll kill you,' I said. 'I will, I'll kill you.'

Modgud raised her pale eyebrows. 'What difference would that make? You still couldn't leave.' She looked at me, almost kindly. 'You'll get used to it, Hel. Everyone does in the end.'

I shook my head fiercely.

We sat silently, lost in the swirling sleet. The only sound was the clashing blocks of ice as they hurtled down the river and the winds that never stopped gusting.

'There's more dead arriving,' she said, pointing. 'Look.'

Coming down the fog road was a shade in the shape

of a woman. A few cooking pots and a spindle clanked behind her.

Modgud ran over and took up her post.

She raised her pale arm, on which no gold bands glittered, and the ghost stopped. She murmured something, then Modgud nodded and stepped aside.

'Pass by.'

The ghost continued slowly on the downward path leading from the bridge.

'Now what am I supposed to do?' muttered the shade. 'Who's chieftain here? Where do I go? This isn't right. I deserve better – I own two farms and five hundred sheep, I –' Her angry voice faded as she vanished beyond the cliffs.

I watched as more and more dead streamed down the long track from Midgard, drawn like moths to the glistening bridge. Some dragged wagon-loads of grave goods behind them, others carried a knife or an axe or a jug. One clutched a broken sword; another a bucket. I felt light-headed. So many dead . . . so many more would arrive. On and on and on –

'You came from – up?' said Modgud. She kept her eyes fixed on the bridge as she spoke.

I nodded.

'Midgard?'

'No, Jotunheim.'

Modgud looked blank.

'Jotunheim. The home of the giants. Like you.'

She shrugged her shoulders. 'Never heard of it.'

'And Asgard. The citadel in the sky where the cursed gods live – the ones who banished me here.'

Modgud lowered her head.

'What's it like up there?' whispered Modgud. 'Under the sky?'

My eyes watered.

'Colour and light.'

'Colour?' said Modgud.

'Like grass is green,' I said.

'I've never seen grass.'

Green like my father's eye. Green like Yggdrasil's leaves. Green like –'Green like – gangrene.'

‘Oh,’ said Modgud. She nodded.

‘Blue – like bruises. Red like blood. Yellow like pus. And it can smell – so sweet,’ I said.

‘Like the dead?’ asked Modgud.

‘No,’ I said. ‘Like the living.’

‘I wouldn’t know about that,’ said the little giantess.

‘How did you get here?’ I asked.

Modgud shrugged. ‘I’ve always been here. Since the worlds began. I know nothing else.’

‘Do you always have to stand guard here?’

‘Yes.’

‘When do you sleep?’

‘The Echoing Bridge screams if anyone alive steps on it,’ she said. ‘I don’t need much sleep –’

She paused, watching a troop of dead warriors drift over Gjoll, bloodstained and hacked, their weapons stilled, their studded helmets dangling. Valhall rejects. Unchosen by the Choosers of the Slain. The unglorious dead. Talk about a club you don’t want to join . . . Would they rampage when they realised their bad fate?

'What will you do now, Queen?'

A million replies raced through my mind, starting with 'Kill the gods' and ending with 'Kill myself.'

'I don't know,' I said.

'The dead need a hall,' said Modgud. 'And so do you.'

A hall. Embla had ranted about a hall.

Modgud waved her bone-white arms. 'It's chaos here,' she said. 'There's no order, no one's in charge, the dead don't know what to do or where to go. We've been waiting for you.'

I am a goddess. And now I was a queen. I couldn't skulk in a cave for eternity.

'I'll build a hall,' I said. 'Beyond those cliffs.' My own place, where no one would tell me what to do. A fortress of stone. A walled stronghold and a great hall within impregnable ramparts. I would carve out a kingdom here, and I would name it . . . The name could come later.

Modgud nodded. 'Come and visit me whenever you like, Hel,' she said. 'It's nice to talk to someone who still has flesh on their body. When you've seen one skull –'

'I keep thinking I hear a dog howling,' I said.

Modgud looked alarmed.

'That's Garm. Don't worry, he's –'

'Where is he? If I call him will he come? I've always wanted a dog –'

'You don't want him,' said Modgud.

'Don't tell me what I want and what I don't.' She was a follower – she had no right to speak to me like that.

'Trust me, you really don't,' said Modgud. Her face was mild, as always. 'He guards one of the other entrances here. He's more monster than dog, actually. He'll rip your head off if you get too close. But don't worry – he's chained up in a cliff cave.'

The image of my wolf brother, frothing in his fetters, came unwelcome into my mind.

'Any other monsters down here I should know about?'

'The dragon, Nidhogg,' said Modgud. 'He lives far below on the Shore of Corpses, twisted around the roots of Yggdrasil. I don't *think* he'd eat you – he likes dead bodies, mainly.'

'Seen him,' I said.

'There's also the black-burnt fire giant, Surt, who rules the southern kingdom across the void. He stands guard at the border in the flames holding a fiery sword – no one who isn't from that land can enter.'

It wasn't hard to cross a fire demon off my calling list.

The full horror of where I was hit me again.

Baldr – I hadn't known how lonely I was until I'd met him. And now –

Just thinking of his name convulsed me. I breathed heavily, then started to cough. The fumes were indescribable in their horror. You'd expect after sharing a cave with a blood-soaked wolf and a poisonous snake (let alone myself) I'd be used to the stench of death.

'It stinks here.'

'Really?' said Modgud. She sniffed the rancid air a few times. 'Can't say I notice.'

I lurched carefully to my feet, trying not to slip on the dripping rocks. I watched the roaming, agitated corpses, flapping about like insects in fire. There was something mesmerising about their swooping motion. What was less hypnotic were their whiny voices and shrill complaints – a great stew of misery.

What a mess. What a horrible mess it was down here. The dead and their angry empty eyes – ugh.

I made my decision then.

Niflheim is the world before the world, the land that exploded into being when time was young and Midgard was silent. I would lift the corners of this ancient chaos and create a new world.

The frightened, mortal gods had imprisoned me and my brothers, but at the End of Days we would break free and rage against them. That's what the prophesy foretold.

Yet until that happy twilight when the doomed gods were destroyed –

I swore three things:

1. I would find a way out.
2. I would see Baldr again.
3. I would be avenged.

20

RAIN-DAMP SLEET-COLD HALL

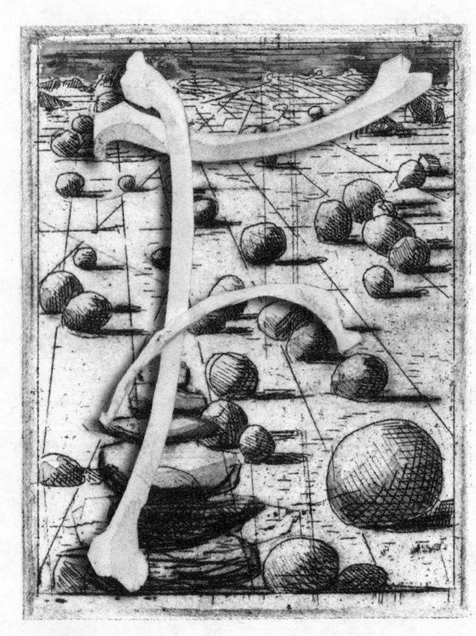

IRST THINGS FIRST. Before I measured out the boundaries of Hel within the blackness of Niflheim, I needed to turn my mind to hall-building. (That's right. I'm going to call my realm Hel. What better name than my own?)

I am a queen; I wanted a hall to rival any in Asgard. There are great riches here to be plundered, if the wealth

I've seen the dead hauling after them is any indication.

Unfortunately (I am so uniquely cursed and unlucky that everything to do with me could begin with that word), I have to design and build my citadel myself. My palace is the first here.

Of course, it needs to be enormous. Greater than any palace in Asgard. There are an awful lot of dead. Why did Odin make his driftwood so weak that they only live for a blink of a raven's eye before cluttering up my kingdom?

How I would love to keep all those wailing shades far, far away from me. If only I could hang a 'Beware of the Monster' sign on my gates, build my hall and lock the doors for eternity.

But I am subject to One-Eye's decree, and I must offer a welcome.

I draw up my list of must-haves.

1. Location. Location. Location. That is key. No building beside a spewing volcano, or sulphurous

swamp, or raging rivers flowing with chewed carcasses. Believe me, places that don't contain at least one of the above are hard to find in Niflheim.

Don't misunderstand me. Even if some sun-dappled meadow with gurgling stream and gambolling sheep *existed* down here, I wouldn't build my hall there. Are you crazy? All beauty does is highlight my ugliness. I prefer to hide in the shadows. There and not there. This hall would be *mine* and I could please myself. A ripple of pleasure pricked me at the thought.

2. My hall must be far from Modgud's bridge. Let my guests get past the Shore of Corpses and the dragon first before they find my gates and slip inside my door, never to leave again.
3. My hall must be far from Nidhogg. The dragon can keep the bloody pit in which he lives. I want nothing to do with the valley where he gnaws on corpses and the great Yggdrasil's roots. I do not

want a dragon for a neighbour. Ditto the howling chained dog that Modgud described. Not in *my* courtyard.

4. My death realm must have high walls; Hel will be a fortress within Niflheim. The ramparts round my kingdom must reach higher than the walls of Asgard. Won't that make the gods rage with jealousy when they hear of the palace I have created?
5. Within those towering walls I will build a hall. Not just any hall, but the largest hall in all the worlds. One-Eye's golden palace will look like a privy beside it. (Mine will smell worse than one, but let's pretend we don't notice.)
6. I like naming things, and I will call my grave mound *Eljudnir*. My Rain-Damp, Sleet-Cold Hall. No *Rose Palace* or *Mount Pleasant* for me. And I'll build icy pitch-black portals named *Corpse Gate* and *Carrion Gate*. I think I've excelled myself with those names. What? You

think I should have called my lovely entrances *Welcome Home* and *Rest Your Feet?* Built a gleaming palace of light and happiness? Ha! I don't want to entice anyone in under false pretences. 'If only we'd known the hideous welcome awaiting us in this dismal hall, we'd have gone elsewhere . . .'

7. Corpse Gate and Carrion Gate, which will lock in the dead forever, must be made of iron, tightly wrought and impassable. I want them oozing, like molton metal, dreadful and oily to the touch. If I can't stop the dead from swarming in, at least my barred gates will keep out any living creatures who might slip past Modgud. I will host no one beyond those I must. If the living want to sneak down here to learn wisdom, they'll get no joy from me. And any wisdom they glean will be too late, as they won't return to Midgard to enjoy it.

8. Inside Eljudnir will be one vast, cavernous space, a banquet hall of halls (just without the banquets, of course). I see chandeliers, hearths, tables laden with jugs and rich hangings on the stone walls. On second thoughts, no hangings – they would only rot and the dead won't appreciate them anyway. That's where the dead will congregate, on benches stretching into infinity. Those mouldy walls will contain an infinite number of bodies. I will also build a lavish bedchamber just for me, curtained off, where no one may enter. That way, I will host the dead but never have to see them. Oh, and treasure rooms. Lots and lots of treasure rooms. And two High Seats, carved and imposing, befitting a great queen. One for me, should I ever decide to receive guests. And one for my love. Because one night Baldr will come to find me – I know he will. And I must be ready for that night.

No kitchen required, obviously. The mead goat that will provide drink can wander about; the dead aren't fussy. And, frankly, I don't care if they are – it's *my* hall and I make the rules. I need no food as I don't have to eat. I just want storerooms for my treasure, and a private bedroom for me. And beyond the hall, stables, ready to receive the horses that have been sacrificed with their masters.

There. My dream home. Not exactly fussy, am I? A gigantic one-bedroom hall with no mod cons.

Perfect.

For a long while I planned and honed my designs, adding a turret here, a palisade there, as I groped my way northwards and downward from Modgud's bridge, pushing through stinging fog and shrieking winds. Building a palace filled my mind. It is astonishing how much plotting and planning dampens sorrow, like ash poured on fire.

At last, after much wandering, I found a wind-swept plain stretching far off into the gloom in all directions.

The air was fetid, and blasting winds blew, and darkness reigned. I had found the spot for my kingdom.

I claimed it for my own.

And then I built my hall, and my kingdom, myself.

I felt power surge through me. I didn't need masons or carters or diggers to carve rock out of the bleak land. I didn't need to hoodwink some poor giant. With one sweep of my arms the rocks and boulders piled themselves atop the other and immense walls loomed above me.

Then fearsome gates bolted with iron. No dragon, no living person, would squeeze through them. The mighty fortifications rose, black and sheer, until they encircled my kingdom.

The restless dead began to gather, waiting.

Then I stepped inside to raise my hall, Eljudnir, from the slime and entrails of the fog world. First, foundations appeared, then stone walls, interlaced with bones. Skulls stacked themselves around empty hearths. (For decoration only, mind. They will never be lit – the dead don't need warmth.) The turf roof thatched itself. Never have I felt more like a goddess as I watched my creation form around me.

You were right to fear me, One-Eye. I too can create order from chaos.

And while I built, all I could think was Baldr Baldr Baldr. Did Baldr know my feverish thoughts? Would he come to rescue me? He was One-Eye's son – maybe his evil father would listen if Baldr pleaded for me. If only. If only . . .

And when my mind was not filled with thoughts of Baldr, I gnawed on revenge. How I could destroy the gods for what they'd done to me. Wild plots and schemes played out in my mind. I had time. I would find a way to lead an army of the dead and ransack Asgard.

When my hall was finished (don't ask how long it took. An hour? Fifty years? It's all the same to me, remember?), I stood on the threshold and surveyed my handiwork.

I admired everything.

And so will you.

Sconces made of skulls hung on the walls. Chandeliers criss-crossed with bones dangled from the roof, festooned with unlit candles – why waste wax on the dead? Stone lamps smoking with fish oil glowed, tiny pools of light in the bitter black, like wolf eyes in moonlight.

I stumbled along the packed-earth floor, trying not to crash into the numberless benches and tables and the low platforms fast against the gold-flecked walls. I'd made two High Seats, richly carved, with side posts, on a raised dais. If anyone ever asked who the other throne was for, I would just say (if I deigned to answer), 'An honoured guest.'

I can't believe I have created all this.

I have a room to myself, curtained off behind the High Seats with a bed hidden behind thick hangings and furnished with grave goods. I've never had a separate place to sleep before.

Picture my richly embellished chamber, a candelabra

burning a hole in the dark. Heavy, embroidered curtains shield my bed, which I call Sorrow. My blanket is Mildew and my bedhangings Hide Me. These fine furnishings will all rot soon enough. No matter. I'll just replace them. As is fitting, the dead bring many offerings, and grave goods are no use to the dead.

Of course Eljudnir is freezing and forbidding. The wind still howls down the roof vent. The air is rank. It is always night, always winter. The terrible gloom never ends: a smothering blanket of fear and solitude and bricked-up misery. It's always wet and draughty. What do you expect? It's the hall of the dead. Death is a serious business.

Don't think I haven't heard my kingdom described as riches and glittering treasures surrounded by foulness, horror, decay, phantoms, mud, filth, stench and squalor. That I am nothing but the queen of a great pestilent burial mound.

That's a bit harsh. A bit ungrateful. I could have let the dead roam the fearsome wastes of

Niflheim. Instead I created a barrow for them in my storm-wracked world.

21

HEL'S HISTORY OF MIDGARD

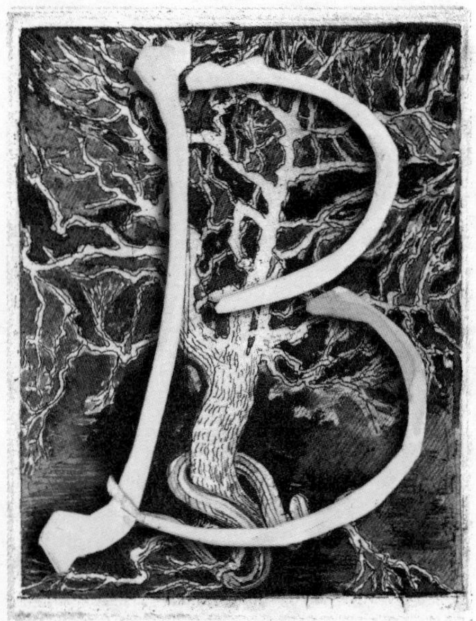

EFORE YOU AND I meet face to face, learn the true history of the world as you know it. Remember what is inscribed here. Repeat it round your fires and in your halls.

The rest is just stuff.

Burning ice and flame. Frost and sparks. No sand. No sea. No sky. No warmth. A great void at the beginning of time.

The giants were first, the oldest inhabitants of the Nine Worlds. The gods, the great tormentors, came afterwards.

Odin and his brothers create Midgard out of the void from the body of the unlucky giant Ymir.

Giants fight gods.

The treacherous gods imprison the frost giants in the ice.

The treacherous gods kidnap my brothers and me and take us to Asgard.

I meet Baldr.

The source of all evil, Odin, hurls me into Niflheim.

Bronze.

Fighting.

Iron.

Fighting.

Steel.

Fighting.

Fighting.

Fighting.

Gunpowder.

Lots of fighting.

The stirrup is invented.

Next the canon.

Snorri Sturluson writes horribly about me in his book called *The Prose Edda*. (Do not read his lies!)

Snorri Sturluson is murdered by his son-in-law – serves him right. He did *not* get a warm welcome from me when his sorry shade shambled down here.

Guns invented – yes!

Plague – yes.

Black death – yes yes yes.

Flying chariots.

Bombs.

Antibiotics – boo.

Vaccination – boo.

Space chariots.

War.

Midgard heats up.

The Frost Giants break free of the ice. Unfortunately, the gods defeat them.

Axe Age, Sword Age.

The Gods die.

End of World.

Have I missed out anything important? I don't think so. When you live forever, you get a perspective on how little most things matter.

You imagine you're special? You're not.

22

THE SERVANT PROBLEM

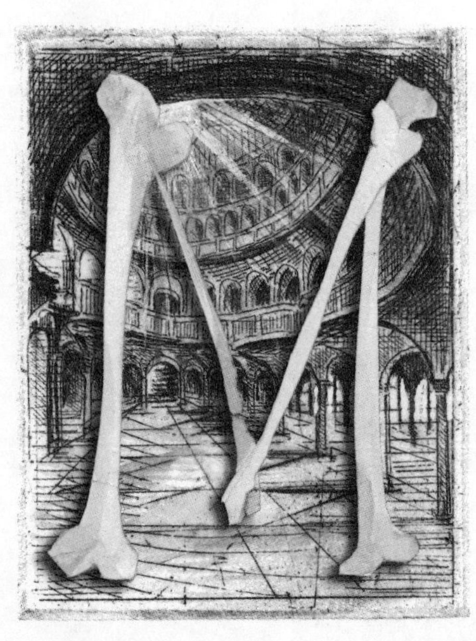

MY DEATH HALL was ready. For a long moment, I took in the silence, Eljudnir's desolation before the pit opened and the dead flowed in. My home would never be empty again. I listened to my breath, soft in the shadows. Fog to fog. My shuffling footsteps echoed in the vastness. My doors would be ajar for eternity, open to the howling wilderness.

I didn't want this peace to end. But since when has anyone cared what I want?

Let them come in.

I was tired and needed to rest after my great labour, but I stumbled towards the massive doors and pushed them open for the first and last –

Wait. What's wrong with that sentence? Not the exhaustion – even gods need to take it easy occasionally –

Why am I opening the doors? I'm the queen. Where are my servants? Who will get out the buckets, unpack the drinking horns, set the holders on the tables, start brewing the mead and kick the goat who at this moment is gnawing on a table leg and splintering it?

Who's going to collect and sort and stack all my grave goods? And change my bedlinen? And freshen my drink? Someone's got to milk the mead goat and fill the horns. That someone isn't me.

I needed a man and maidservant.

When I lived with my mother in Jotunheim, we had servants. I had no idea how they came to live with us, or where they came from. I never asked. They were slaves, and beneath my notice.

How was I to find servants down here?

I sat on my uncomfortable throne – I would seek out cushions from my tribute as soon as possible – and watched the dead pour through the open doors and spill into my hall, stumbling as they crossed the threshold, ducking their rotting heads and stooping at the entrance, accustomed as most of them are to low hovels. (I told you I get the riff-raff.) It's like emptying a bottomless chamber pot; a river of corpses which never stops flowing, the way the dead slop in here. They shivered in the cold, dripping with hoar frost.

The rich ones brought their tributes of gold and jewels and ivory and swords. The poor held tight to their useless wooden cups and needles and buckets. I took it all. Every night down here will be my birthnight, a feast of never-ending gifts. I'd never had a gift before. I lurched off my throne and grabbed an arm bracelet, heavy with bright gold, then another and another. I sieved through the growing pile of grave goods, tossing aside the broken pottery and soapstone bowls and dried fish, snatching up earrings and a silver buckle. I snatched like Fen after rats.

I placed the jewels on my wrists and fingers, pinned a filigree brooch to my robe while the newly arrived, bewildered and angry, flailing, smelly and grumbling, milled about the ghastly hall seeking their place.

'Sit anywhere,' I said. (Except next to me, of course.) 'There is no rank here.' Oh, how they wailed and gnashed at that.

I eyed the dead for likely servant material.

What are my requirements?

1. Ugly.
2. Quiet.
3. No one decomposing.

Like I said, I'm not Miss Fussy.

Number one was easy. Two and three seemed impossible.

I saw wraiths and cadavers, decaying and freshly buried; fretful spirits fluttering about like greasy shadows; and corpses with peeling skin and maggots dripping from their heads.

Every body was worse than the next. Most were old. And bony. And putrefying. All talking at me. I thought the dead would come in quietly. Sit down. Be still. Act dead.

But oh no. The din was horrendous. Jabbering, querulous voices. Moaning. Yelling. Gathering around my High Seat, shrieking and screaming like stuck pigs.

The shrieks of those fathers whose sons were too mean to bury them with gold and who discovered they'd arrived here with a wooden bowl and a dented axe.

The stupid slave girls who'd volunteered to be sacrificed, thinking that if they follow their chieftain in death they'll be his wife here in Hel. *Where* do they get these ideas? Ladies, it isn't going to happen. Save yourselves. Don't volunteer for any funeral pyres. Everyone journeys to me alone.

'Have I been chosen by Freyja instead of Odin to live in *her* hall?' asked one pudgy, bloodstained warrior, looking around in amazement. He gazed at me uneasily, seated on my throne, my silver hair exploding around my lead face, a blanket covering my legs.

'Is this Asgard?'

'Does this look like Asgard to you?' I asked.

His eyes widened.

'I thought every warrior who fell in battle went to Valhall!' he howled.

'Well, you thought wrong,' I said. 'Only the best and greatest warriors go to Valhall. Which obviously excludes *you*.'

His fellow warriors shuffled unhappily.

I braced myself.

'Where's the banquet? Where's the never-ending ale in the curved horns?' they screamed. 'Where's the roast pork and the maidens serving?'

The disappointment and fury of the first-class arrivals, the kings with their servants and animals aboard their iron-shielded ships, when they end up here. Just as stinky as the grimiest thrall, the filthiest troll. I wanted to laugh.

One stormed up to me, haughty and full of majesty in his silken tunic with gold buttons and fur hat, his slaves dragging in carts and wagons and jewels and bright swords.

'I demand you receive me as a great lord,' he boomed.

'Or what?' I said. All the timber and amber and rings didn't alter the fact that he was – er – dead.

'There's some mistake,' others protested.

Nope.

I covered my ears, ignoring them all. The corpses buzzed and whined around me like angry wasps.

'Where's my throne?'

'I'm not sitting with him!'

'Don't touch that jug – it's mine.'

'You stink!'

'Give me that –'

'I want to go home . . .'

'What am I doing here?'

'My sister, the greedy cow, she kept my ivory comb!'

'It's not fair –'

Then out of the gloom I saw an old crone, carrying an empty gold plate, coming towards me.

An ancient man shuffled beside her, holding a knife and a cup.

I watched them approach. I am not sure that *approach* is the right word. Were they actually moving? It was hard to say. Time slips away here. Time is of no importance. I was having to learn this.

But one thing became clear as inch by inch they came closer to my throne. Both of these grey-haired, filthy thralls were alive.

The hordes of the dead parted to let them through.

'We've been waiting for you, mistress,' said the crone. Her thin, grey plaits twisted beneath a dirty cap the colour of dung. Her words fell out of her mouth in long, slow syllables, like pus oozing from a wound.

'We've been waiting forever,' said the old hag spawn.

His matted tufts of white hair stuck up on his bald head like horns.

They had no names, so I named them: Ganglot the Lazybones and Ganglati the Slowpoke.

'Here is your plate – Starving,' said Lazybones.

'Here is your knife – Famine,' said Slowpoke.

'Here is your cup – Thirst,' they said together.

Fine dining was evidently not going to be their forte.

When I write that they said these words, I have written them down as sentences. That's not how they talked. Slowpoke and Lazybones spoke as if they died after every word, and then slowly came back to life to speak one more word before dying again. It took them a day to cross a room, a night to cross back. They moved so slowly they almost appeared not to budge. In the time it took them to set down my plate, knife and cup, I could have staggered up the fog road back to Midgard (if only). Watching them lift an arm to wipe their noses on their crusty sleeves could take an eternity.

Not exactly first choice for servants.

But they, like Modgud, were alive. And I loathe the dead even more than I hate the living. I too can only move slowly. And in a world without time, what's the rush?

23

YOUR WOLF-GRACIOUS HOST

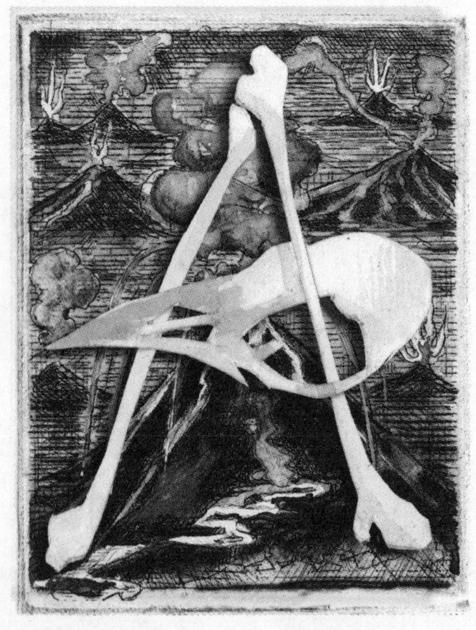

ALL RIGHT. I'M feeling chatty. I'll throw you a bone, so to speak.

I'll tell you what happens when you die. How it all works. Yes, the greatest secrets of all. So there will be no more need to seek spell songs to raise the dead to make them talk. I'm spilling the beans.

Deal? Good.

You die. 'Wah wah wail wail.' (That's you by the way.) Don't kid yourself. No one will miss you.

If you're shoved into a grave mound, you rot and stagger down to me looking pretty rough and smelling worse.

If your body is burned, you waft to me in spirit form. Either way you all end up pouring down the Hel Road.

At the bridge between the worlds, Modgud checks you're dead, asks your name and lineage, and quietly you cross over the frosty river and into my melancholy world of sleet and weeping darkness. There's no turning back.

The dead whose bodies have burned on pyres pass through a wall of flames. Smoke meets smoke, and the last remnant of their mortal selves blows off, like sparks from a sword being burnished, like ash from sputtering wood.

Fading, fading, gone. Poof.

But, once across the bridge, everything changes. The yowling they make, you'd think they were the first who'd ever died. Well, you're not, so get over it.

I, your reluctant and wolf-gracious host, will greet you. Greet in the sense that I'll allow you into my windy hall. Please do not look for any more recognition because expectation will always be disappointed. Don't imagine you can please me. *No one* can please me. *NO ONE*.

Hopefully, you're bringing lots of gifts. Remember, grave goods are a tribute for your new lord – me. *You* will not need anything with which you've been buried.

Please note: I have enough wooden serving platters, buckets, spindles and broken swords to last for eternity. I like goblets, carved ivory animals and brooches. You can't have too many of those. And gold. I love gold.

In fact, let me repeat: NO MORE WOODEN PLATTERS. I know some mortals make greedy lists of the gifts they desire when they marry, and circulate this among their kin and their friends and followers. Here's my list: just gold and silver.

And, please, no looms. No one's weaving down here.

Leave looms behind. No need to lug a loom down the fog road. Load your wagon with treasure instead.

Treasure. Sadly, all too rare. Too many relatives planning to place that gold armband in the grave, snatch it back at the last moment and substitute – for shame – a broken old pot. Or a rusty axe instead of a jewelled spear. No wonder there's so much shrieking and gnashing down here when the dead sift through their possessions and discover a pile of junk.

My entrance requirements are minimal – that you're dead.

That's it. Modgud, my bouncer, lets everyone into the club. We're not exclusive. No VIP section. No velvet ropes.

Welcome.

My gate slams on your heels. Your name passes out of use like withered grass.

Goodbye. Good riddance.

You who are full of easy time, gloating and careless, singing in your chains –

Remember.

Everyone is mine at the end.

•

While we're on the subject of death journeys, here's a useful tip. Pack your jewels and inlaid shields and gold arm rings and ditch the rest. Because you would not believe the junk the deceased bring with them. Hams. Sheep's heads. Apples. Mead buckets. Why? Did they think it was going to be one non-stop feast here? One eternal party with dancing bears and fighting? Swords, axes, brooches, pots, coins, cauldrons, grindstones, helmets, sickles, stools, goblets, horses, dogs, slaves, hawks. Thanks awfully for the silver spoon and I can always use another gold ring, but no thanks for the broken pots and bent swords.

When the corpses find out that I take everything valuable they've brought for tribute – which is only fair, mind you; they are living here for eternity, the guests who never leave, the guests who stink like long-dead fish – they yell and scream even more. But what were they hoping to buy – a new body?

Once I've grabbed what I want, the gold and jewels to decorate my hall and fill my treasure rooms, I have the trash flung outside. Let them fight over it. They drift about rustling like dry leaves, gripping some old cup as if their life – ha ha – depended on it. I tell you, it's like a grisly bring-and-buy sale held on a reeking rubbish tip.

That One-Eye. What a mean trick he played on his followers, telling them that every man who died in battle would enter Valhall with as much wealth as he had on his pyre. What a death jest. What a liar.

Those Valkyries nabbed everyone they needed in the time before time. Valhall's doors are shut. The benches are full. No one can budge up at the nightly feast.

Hero, you're too late. *I'm* your hostess in the afterdeath.

Hard luck.

Bad fate.

Yeah, whatever.

You might as well drop that sword now and be a farmer. Forget the battle heroics and do something else. Because, whatever happens, you're coming to me.

Sorry to be the one to break the news, but at least this way you'll be prepared for the inevitable rude welcome Chez Hel.

Some of you decide to stick around in your grave-mound, sitting blank-eyed and staring on your high chair, throttling any of the living who dare to break in to steal your treasure. Or, worse, you go haunting your former homes, savaging the sheep or scaring the Hel out of your family.

If the living are wise, they'll cover up any mirrors or water in their homes, in case the dead souls are drawn to their reflections and sneak inside to hang around Midgard a bit longer. I honestly don't know why they bother. Is it really so much fun terrifying your family by creeping up the stairs or popping out of chests? What good does that do? You're still dead. Face it: however much they loved you in Midgard, they really don't want you lurching about now.

But even you restless ones finally descend to my dark kingdom, after those who have carved your name upon your gate posts have gone, and your memory slowly vanishes from the worlds. Then you'll drift down the fog road to me.

The mists of Niflheim and my beckoning voice will fill your grave barrow. Slowly you'll sink to my world beneath the worlds. And ultimately you'll join the oldest corpses, who flit like smoke. They stare with glaring eyes from which all speculation is banished, as one so-so poet once wrote. The dead live here in an everlasting past. Then present. Then ...

However, there is no point in complaining. I never listen. I just don't care. You're not happy? Go somewhere else. There's a nice dragon I know who always needs feeding ...

I've told you too much. Far more than I intended. But storytellers get carried away. Words spill from unlocked word hoards.

Want to know more about my life here? Actually, I don't care what you want. You would do well to listen until I am no longer willing to speak.

24
PUTRID TIME

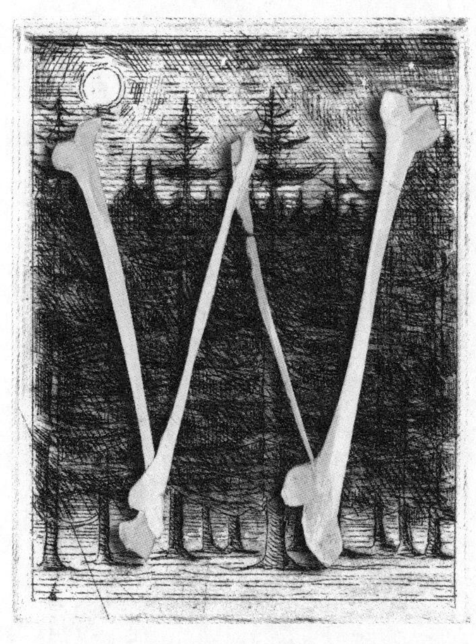

HEN YOU HAVE ALL the time in the world, how do you live knowing that each moment will pass exactly as the one before? And the one now. And the one after. Each slow drip of putrid time, on and on and on and on and on and on and on and –

How do you bear it? Even when you're queen?

When you live in a stinking pitch-black world, a living

being imprisoned inside a massive grave mound filled with the howling dead, you become a thing more dead than living. If beauty annihilates thought, then I have nothing but thoughts.

I keep alive because of . . . *him*. Imagining a life with him. Living with Baldr in my mind. Our happiness. Our joy. We talk. We laugh. I remember when I heard him singing, his mellifluous voice. I remember his beautiful mouth.

This is my hideous, horrible life:

I slump on my High Seat. I lie on my damp bed. I visit my treasure room. I drink. I brood. I watch my slow servants.

HERE –

IS –

GANGLATI –

BRINGING –

ME –

A –

GLASS –

OF –

WINE.

NOW –

HE –

IS –

PICKING –

UP …

You get the idea. Wanna trade places?

Didn't think so.

Once I watched the dead throwing a ball, using a seal's head glowing with heat, with flying sparks and fat dripping like tallow. That I had never seen before and I was diverted.

Then they stopped, the head decayed, and nothingness resumed.

Sometimes the bodies take up drinking horns and hold contests. They pour mead into their gaping mouths, which leaks through what flesh remains and dribbles onto the ground. The newly dead take time to shuck off such mortal pursuits. I watch them drink and drink, oblivious that their putrefying bodies and jutting ribs hold no liquid. They soon tire.

Bet you can't wait to join us.

Every now and then, when I think I will go mad, I listen to the stories told by skalds, for the brief time they can remember their sagas, declaring ancient histories of mortals and gods and giants.

Even the dead cease their relentless drone when a newly arrived skald stands in the middle of my hall and tells how the world began or how Odin sacrificed an eye for wisdom (the dunce).

I don't like poets, with their weasel words.

I've had enough of being described as monstrous – and worse. The mead of poetry sours when poured down my throat. Not surprising, since poetry was a gift to people from One-Eye. Any wonder I hate it? I will keep my own history. I can bind time better than any.

But, mostly, I hate. I have time – oh yes, more time than anyone, god or mortal – to stew. I am not time-fettered. The memories of the dead fade, until even their names vanish. But mine have sharpened. I live for vengeance. I breathe it in great gasping gulps. I dream of vengeance, feed on vengeance, let bile fill my veins. I drink poison, hoping others die.

I warm myself with plans and schemes. Will any giants avenge my kidnap and steal Thor's splotchy, buck-toothed daughter, Thrud? Wouldn't that serve old red-beard right? Or what about Freyja's simpering Hnoss, with her fat legs and pouty lips? Let her try living in my mother's cave for a bit. See how long she'd last . . .

And so my thoughts circle round and round.

But, more than that, so much more than that, night after night, year after year, century after century, I think about Baldr. If only I could see him again. My thoughts about him are infinite. I know that he loves me. I know that I love him. I've never loved anyone before. When I feel I am drowning in despair he is the one thing that keeps me from hurling myself in Nidhogg's way.

I lie on my dank bed and close my eyes, my pillow scrunching and crackling under my head. I think of Baldr's beauty. His kindness. His loving eyes. The way he picked me up and spun me round. He has got under my skin and into my heart. I can shut out the misery of the dead next door and be alone with my thoughts. I pull the bed hangings tight across, and dream of love.

Baldr. My lovely Baldr. How can I lure him here? He needs to die. But gods don't die. Maybe, just maybe, One-Eye will send him, seeking wisdom, and I'll find a way to keep him. What a wonder that would be, a god in Hel. How the gods would suffer without him. How I would rejoice with him.

I need to cling to something, some small hope of happiness, of freedom, while I lie here rotting in my prison beneath the worlds.

I am low in spirits. I think I will visit Modgud.

25
MODGUD

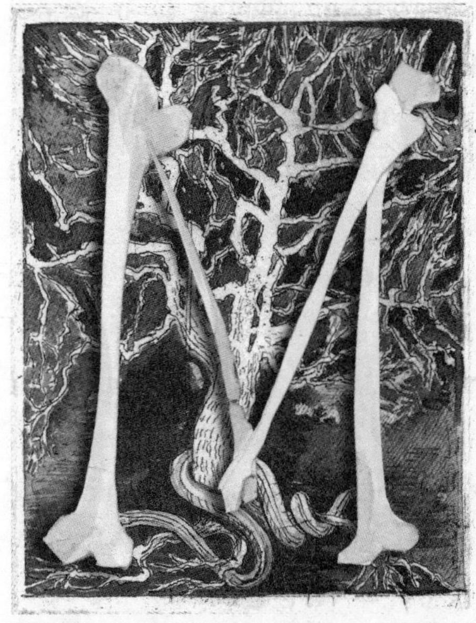

ODGUD ISN'T A *friend*. I'm the Goddess of the Underworld; I have no friends. I don't want any friends. I am fine by myself. I am cradled by hate and fury; I need no one. But, every millenia or so, I leave my hall and journey to Gjoll, the boundary river between the living and the dead, to see her.

The giantess always looks the same. She does not age,

does not grow taller. Time is still for her, as it is for all here. She is always pleased to see me. I think she is the only creature I have ever known who is.

We sit by the glowing bridge on the riverbank, watching the shadows. The ground is freezing and the wind moans over the blasted hills. Neither of us speaks. The dead still stream across, silently, a never-ending line of arrivals. The fog road, dotted with fire, the last vestiges of the world of the living, looks so close, and yet for me it could be a million miles away.

'So how goes it?' says Modgud. Her watchful eyes are tiny pinpricks of light.

I have no idea where she learns this language. So far as I know she never talks to the dead other than to ask their name and lineage. And yet she speaks words and phrases I have never heard.

'My hall is filling,' I say. 'It's awful.'

'Tell me about it,' says Modgud, sighing. 'It's a non-stop procession of corpses down here.'

'So much for those whining poets singing

warnings that guests mustn't overstay their welcome, as loved becomes loathed if they sit too long at another's hearth.'

'The dead don't listen,' says Modgud.

'Once they find you, they stay forever,' I say. 'Hint all you like; they don't budge. Yank 'em out, show 'em the door, they slip right back in.'

'Why don't you line every bench with red-hot pokers?' says Modgud. She is smiling.

I grimace. 'They'd still make themselves comfy.'

I'm finding it difficult to speak of why I've come back to Gjoll after so many winters have passed. What could I say? Instead I ask:

'Why do you stay here? Why don't you leave?'

Modgud looks astonished.

'And go where?'

'Anywhere,' I say.

'I can't,' says Modgud. 'I'm the Warden of the Bridge.'

There was another long silence. We listened to the

pounding water and the wind-blown shades passing over the bridge.

'Even if I could, where would I go?' says Modgud.

'Have you ever tried?'

Modgud's salt-white face pales.

'No!'

She looked around, as if we might be overheard.

'OK. Once. Oh, I was terrified. That flames would consume me. That my body would crumble into dust. I've never been above. I'd like to see Midgard. Even just for a moment.'

'Go on, then,' I say. 'I won't tell. Who are you guarding this place from, anyway? You think the living are going to stage a mass invasion?'

Modgud's face droops.

'I can't cross the bridge any more than you can.'

I'm not sorry. Who was it who said that misery loves company? They were right.

Modgud picks up a stone and lobs it into the raging river.

'Why did you do that?' I ask.

Modgud shrugs. 'I like the *plop* sound.'

I pick up a small black rock. It feels smooth and heavy in my hands. It is good to touch something that isn't dead, even if it isn't alive. Something that doesn't hold a death stench.

On impulse I hurl it into the river. The rock bounces and splashes before sinking in the torrent.

We sit on the steep bank and lob rocks into the water. I don't understand this game, but the plop of the stones in the river is strangely soothing.

Plop.

Plop.

Plop.

Plop plop.

I could do this for nights.

Plop.

If the dead were startled to see their queen lobbing rocks into the water, they did not show it.

A shivering corpse meanders across the shining

bridge. Modgud drops her pebbles, holds up her arm and the spectre pauses.

'Before you go further,' she says, 'your name and your lineage.'

'I was Helgi, son of Sigurd the Abrupt,' says the dead man.

Modgud nods.

'Pass by,' she says, lowering her gleaming arm.

The corpse vanishes into the vapour.

'Slow night for once,' she says, sitting down again beside me on the riverbank.

'What news of the worlds above?'

Modgud shrugs.

'Many warriors have passed here, more than usual. There is much fighting.'

The longing to say Baldr's name out loud fills me.

I won't say anything, I vow.

'Have you ever been in love?' I ask.

'I don't think so,' says Modgud.

I wait.

But Modgud does not ask me.

Suddenly I feel that if I don't speak his name I will burst.

'There's someone who loves me,' I blurt. 'And someone whom I love.'

Of course I didn't say that. I hide my feelings, my true self. No one may see them.

But I want so much to say his name, to have his name fill my mouth.

'I'm in love,' I say. The words stick on my tongue like wet clay.

I instantly regret it. If I could recall the words and lock them back up I would.

'What is love?' says Modgud.

She's asking *me?*

'Love is when you can't think about anything except the one,' I said. 'It is aching with love-longing. It is to have no thoughts in your head but about them. What would they think, what would they like, why aren't they here, who are they with, over and over until you are driven mad and you would kill everyone in the world if it meant they lived.'

Modgud's white-lashed eyes widen. She shakes her head.

'No,' she says. 'Who would I love?'

And then it all flooded out. I told her everything. I'd been bursting to say his name. Baldr. Baldr. Baldr.

'Even I have heard that name,' says Modgud.

'Is there any way – do you suppose I might – do you think I'll ever see Baldr again?'

'Why don't you ask the seeress?' said Modgud.

Seeress? Seeress?

I thought I had met everyone there was to meet down here.

'What seeress? Where can I find her?'

'Gods brought her body and buried her deep in that grave mound by your eastern door,' said Modgud. 'She remembers the age before the beginning of the worlds and can see far into the future.'

After all this time she mentions a seeress? I could

not believe I'd been down here for so long and had not known that she existed.

'Actually it's best to leave her be: seeresses hate being disturbed,' said Modgud. 'Especially this one.'

What did I care what a long-dead seeress liked or didn't like? She could tell me what my future held. What's the point of being queen if you can't have your own way?

26

THE SEERESS

STUMBLE SLOWLY through the sleet over the frozen ground to her grave mound by the hall's east door. I'd passed it many times and never wondered who was buried there. The nameless dead, swirling like smoke, scatter as I step through them. It's like walking through mist, pushing through the massed cobwebbed ghosts.

Her mound is ringed with stones, in the shape of a ship. Modgud says she's grumpy, but I can force her up. The great seeress, older than time, can surely tell me what I so desperately need to know.

I mutter a few charms, sprinkle herbs on her mound. There is a stirring, and a clinking, and slowly the gleaming spectre rises out of her grave. She looms above me, clutching her staff. Her face is chalk white, twisted in rage. The charm belt about her waist shudders and chimes as she trembles. The air smells ranker, and feels colder, with her there.

'Who forces me up?' she moans, her eyes tightly closed. 'Why have you brought sorrow upon me? It's death to mortals to raise the dead. On you and your children will be my curse for –'

'Open your eyes, Seeress,' I snap.

'You can't make me,' she said.

'Wanna bet?' I say.

Her milky eyes flutter open. She grimaces.

'Ugh. You're so ugly.'

I resist, but the taunt hits me, like an axe to my belly.

'Have you seen yourself?' I hurl back. It's quite something when even a corpse calls you ugly.

The seeress smiles, showing her shattered teeth. She gleams in the murk like a spluttering candle. The stink of the henbane buried with her wafts towards me.

'What do you want, daughter of a pig?' she moans, shaking her bald head, so that the wisps of twisted hair still clinging to her scalp shudder like dangling worms.

One advantage the dead have over the living is that you can't threaten them.

'Make it quick, Hel.'

I do nothing at speed, but I hesitate because . . . there is something familiar about her. Her harsh voice. Her insults . . .

'How do you know my name?'

The seeress hovers above me, crackling with hate.

'I am long dead; I'm not daft. I named you myself.'

It's my mother.

I start to shake.

I stare at the spectre, and try to connect this enraged corpse with Angrboda, my gorgeous mum. The anger is the same; the body . . . different.

There's a lot I could say. I say none of it. I feel a rush of pleasure that I am alive, however grimly, and she is dead.

'What does my future hold?' I ask, finally.

'You don't want to know,' she says, waving her knotted staff.

I want to scream at her.

'Obviously I do, or I wouldn't have summoned you,' I pause. 'Mother.'

The seeress snorts.

'What's going to happen to me?' I say, kicking away one of the stones marking her mound. I'm glad to see her flinch.

'Nothing good,' she gloats. 'You brought me nothing but misery.'

'And you?' I say. 'What do you think you brought me?

Why didn't you rescue us? You didn't even try.'

'I was dead,' said Angrboda. 'The gods killed me after they kidnapped you.'

'That's no excuse,' I screech.

'You disgust me,' she said. 'I will say no more.'

'And the End of Days? How long must I wait for my revenge?'

'See my lips?' she said. 'They're sealed.'

'Will anyone live afterwards?'

'That's for me to know and you to find out. As you will, Wolf's Sister. I am no longer prepared to speak. Now let me sleep.' Slowly she begins to sink back into the ground.

'Wait. You owe me this much. Will I see Baldr again?'

Her pale lips sneer.

'You will. I don't want to speak and I will say no more.'

For a moment I cannot breathe. I clutch my hands to my face. I feel as if a million suns have come out at once. But each answer gives rise to another question.

If he comes to me here, it means he has to die. But how could Baldr die? And yet, and yet, if dead, Baldr would be here, with me, forever. He would be mine. The slow crawl of my nights would be over, if only he were here to share them.

But if I saw him when he were alive . . . who knew what that meant?

Questions spill from my mouth. 'Will I see him here or above? Will he be alive or dead?'

'That's all I'm telling you,' snaps the seeress.

Is it any wonder I'm not the jolliest of goddesses?

'What happens at the End of Days? My brothers will be in at the kill – but what about me?'

The seeress glares at me, and begins to dissolve.

'That depends on the mortal hero who will come.'

More riddles.

'What mortal hero? Come where? *Here?* How will I know him?'

Why could she not speak plainly?

'I don't want to speak and I will say no more.'

I am full of rage and move to strike her.

'You will obey me, you – you – horrible hag!' I shriek. 'Tell me what I want to know. Spit it out, Mother.'

'We'll meet again when Fenrir and Jormungand break free and all the creatures of darkness storm the citadel of the gods and destroy them,' she says. 'When the world ends in ice and fire. Till then I . . .' Her remaining words are lost to me as she sinks back into her mound.

I think . . . I think I won't ever raise her again.

27

LIFE IS HEL

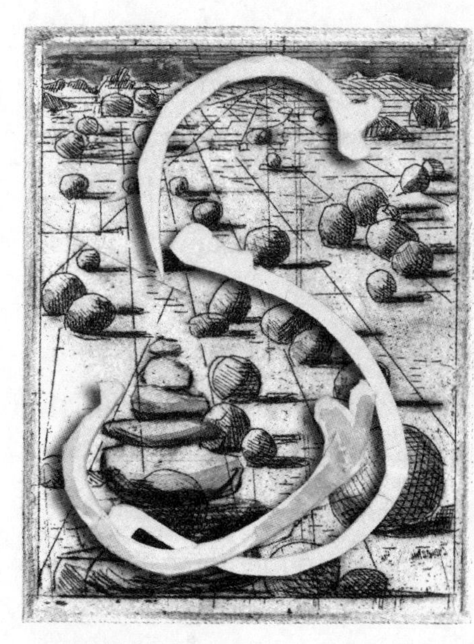

O WHAT'S IT LIKE being Queen of the Dead I hear you ask?

Fabulous! A laugh a minute, best job in the world, everyone wants to be me . . .

What a stupid question. What do you think it's like?

Here's why I'd rather be where you are, and you be where I am.

1. It's lonely.
2. It's crowded.
3. It's smelly.
4. It's boring. Nothing changes except once every thousand years or so – who bothers to track time? – when something interesting happens. By interesting I mean – well, you'll find out.
5. My abominable guests never leave.
6. The servant problem. I'm a queen and I live in a hall larger than any of the gods'. Yet my servants are impossible. They're slow. They're lazy. They're insolent. 'What are you going to do, kill me?' said one corpse, before he was dispatched to Nidhogg's mercies.
7. No one ever says thank you. You build the hall, you brew the mead, you let them through the gate and – no one is ever pleased to see you. Ever. Is it any wonder I look sad and grim? Wouldn't you if you'd been banished to the underworld for no fault of your own and

forced to spend eternity with corpses? Too right you would.

8. No one treats death like an adventure. No one makes the best of things, as I have had to. They moan and whimper, despite the welcome I offer, which is insulting if you think about it. All that work, all that effort to build a hall, offer mead, and my guests would rather be anywhere but here.
9. And please don't get me started about the headless corpses staggering around Midgard when they should be locked up down here. They're the ones who die into the hills, who aren't content to sit in their grave mounds and gloat over their treasure. Oh no, they have to rampage around their old home, haunting and killing till the living dig them up and deal with their angry souls by chopping off their heads and burning them. Why not make things easier for you and yours and just come straight down the fog road? Cut out the middleman, as people say.

I have to acknowledge that the newly dead are never very keen about being dead. But don't blame me. I'm not killing people, remember? I'm only the . . . hostess. Not with the mostess, that's for sure, zero out of five stars in every survey, but in my own small way I try to make my guests – well, if not comfortable, then not *too* uncomfortable.

Just think of me as the proprietor of a haunted hotel where no one ever checks out.

On the plus side:

1. I am the best-looking person here. You know what they say about the one-eyed man being king in the land of the blind? Well, in Hel *anyone* with flesh on their bones has it over the skeletons. Actually, anyone *alive* is number one. My bottom half is hideous, but compared to the rest I'm the Goddess Freyja times a hundred. I even get wolf-whistled. (Yeah, by actual wolves.)

2. My hall is stuffed with precious gifts. I may live in a dung heap but it's girdled with gold.
3. I'm the boss. Whatever I say, goes. Even One-Eye can't order me around here.
4. I never have to see my family again.
5. Everyone smells worse than I do.
6. No one recoils –

Wait a moment. I am interrupted . . .

Oh gods. Just what I don't need. Not *another* shaman chanting charms, trying to yank spirits back up to the living and taking on the shape of a reindeer or a bird to sneak into my kingdom. Frankly, I prefer the birds to the snake forms those sons of mares also assume. (And I'll draw a veil over the time some poor idiot took on a whale's body and blundered down here, though that provided a lot of fish oil for the lamps.)

Sorted. One more shaman who won't be bothering me again.

Idiot.

Let this be a warning to you.

People are always trying to raise the dead and get their help, hoping the ghosts will teach them spells or reveal what is to come.

'Awake at the doors of the dead, Mother,' some feckless son will mewl.

And that poor spirit, safely passed into the earth and long gone from the world of men, will have to heave her weary bones and obey.

The living like tormenting the dead. The dead know the future, what is fated for those whom fate can still trouble. That's a cruel gift, since it's too late for them.

So the living try to rouse them and make them tell secrets, reciting runes to drag the ghost back into the body. The old wood-stick-carved-with-runes-under-a-corpse's-tongue trick, to make it talk … Pulses, can I advise against this? The newly dead HATE being yanked back into the bonds of their bodies and won't thank you for disturbing them.

In fact, they'll curse you. I don't care if they do,

because I certainly don't care about them or about you. But it disturbs the peace here. And I don't like being disturbed.

So don't say you weren't warned.

Such a bad idea to summon the dead. Really. Don't do it. They'll only get angry, and insult you, and foretell your death just to serve you right.

Trust me. You don't want to know which day is the one decreed for you to journey from life to death. If you know, you'll watch it coming closer and closer. It's gonna happen, okay? Just live your brief, precious life. You'll find out soon enough when the Fates have snipped your thread.

And as for trying to get down here before your time is up? NOOOOOOO! Even worse. You'll be lost between the worlds and that's a dangerous place to be.

What's the rush?

You'll be here soon enough.

28

DANCE MACABRE

ONIGHT, FOR THE first time ever, candles flicker in my rain-damp hall. The hearths are lit and whale oil glows in the lamps, casting rays of light in the watery darkness. (Unfortunately, because misfortune tails me everywhere, that also means I can see my guests.) A poet waits before my throne, bony hands gripping his harp, about to play and sing at my command. Barrels full of shining mead stand brimming and ready. Drinking horns are slowly being filled. Gold rings flash on the benches and tables and fresh rushes have been piled on the fetid floor.

I am holding a feast.

Modgud had suggested it after I told her all about my evil mother.

'A feast?' I said.

'A hall-warming feast.'

'You mean a hall-cooling feast.'

'Call it what you like,' said Modgud. 'You've built a kingdom, raised a hall, welcomed so many guests. It's always so gloomy and sad here. Why not?'

I'd heard tell of feasts. Of course I'd never been to one. But I had mead. I had gold. We could have singers and skalds like Egil, son of Bald-Grim, and Audun the Plagiarist, reciting poetry and telling sagas. I probably had enough plates and cups ripped from graves to lay before twenty thousand.

That brought me up short. Who would my

company be? Assorted skeletons and corpses . . . Not exactly crème de la crème. Not exactly a who's who of humanity.

'Would you come?' I asked.

Modgud shook her head.

'I can't leave the bridge. But you'll visit again and tell me all,' she said. 'What you wore. How your hall was decorated. That way we will enjoy it twice.'

A chance to be a tiny bit happy.

Why not? I thought. *Why not.*

So many silver spoons, so many bowls, so much gold piling up. Why not make an effort just once?

So here I am, covered in jewels, wearing furs and fine, soft robes threaded with gold and silver, swishing to the ground, enduring the *plinky plink* of a harp and watching my guests trying to dance without ripping each other's rotting arms off. My servants, Slowpoke and Lazybones, move at their sepulchral pace filling mead horns.

Am I having a good time?

Do you really have to ask?

The glutton, unless he stands guard, will eat himself to death. No fear of gluttony here. No one will be racing for the buffet table and stuffing their faces. It's a feast, but no food is offered. And yet the visitors will never, ever, leave.

What am I doing?

The skeleton skald rises to start his poem. That will pose a challenge – a skald is meant to proclaim poems to honour his chieftain and his glorious deeds. I allow myself a tiny smile as I wonder how the poet will contrive to praise me. For what? My beauty? I don't think so. My kindness? Don't make me laugh. And which great deeds exactly will he hymn? My grave-goods snatching? My pitiless reign? My kidnap by the gods and my exile here? Wait, I've got it! My shapely legs, the envy of women everywhere.

Yes, I'm definitely entering into the party spirit.

It's far better, truthfully, that I am my own skald. They say all rulers must have one, for who else will sing their praises or scold them for their errors? Who else will write their names upon the gates when they are gone? Yet my fame does not concern me. I alone, of all goddesses, am known to all. *No one* wants to know me better. I need no greedy poet to spread my fame. Somehow I don't think you'll forget me, poems or no.

But for tonight I am content to listen. Audun the Plagiarist starts with the saga of how the giants created the worlds – good move. If he'd begun by praising the gods, I'd have had his skull.

The dead gradually cease their dancing and gibbering, and pause to listen. My brooding hall is silent, except for the poet describing how Midgard was created out of the great void from the body of the giant Ymir. Yes, you heard right, a *giant*. Midgard was made from his skin. The sea from his blood. The mountains and rocks from his bones, and the trees from his hair. Look up! See the sky? That came from Ymir's skull. Those little fluffy clouds? Ymir's brains. (So every single one of you, still living, walks on a giant, eats food grown from a giant, bathes in water from a giant, lives surrounded by a giant.)

Just saying.

And who created the world of gods and people? asks the skald. Who was big enough, mighty enough, to kill a giant like Ymir, hurl his body around the cosmos and carve out Midgard from the slime with his flesh and blood and bones? Why, none other than Odin, son of the giantess Bestla, shaped the world. And using the body from his own kinsman on his mother's side. That's a family gathering I wouldn't want to be at, he sings.

'So where's Uncle Ymir? Haven't seen him lately.'

'Uhhmm, dead.'

'What do you mean, dead?'

'Dead. We chopped him up . . .'

I am actually enjoying this poet's words, telling the tale of my giant ancestors. Even the corpses grin. Though that could just be rigor mortis.

And then music strikes up, the benches are pushed back and suddenly everyone is dancing and stomping. Someone sweeps me off my throne and before I know what I'm doing I'm dancing too. Everyone wants to dance with me. I drink a horn of mead, then another, and another, admiring my glittering hall as I whirl from partner to partner, closing my eyes and pretending that each one is Baldr, the music roaring in my ears and filling my soul.

Maybe my life isn't all bad.

More mead! More dancing! I want more, more –

Then I hear Garm baying, louder than I've ever heard before. Crazed and frantic with fury, his yowls reverberate from his cliff cave down to my hall. I hear him straining and lunging against his chains, aching for the kill.

Then hoof beats. The pounding of an eight-legged horse is like no other. In Hel, it sounds like thunder. The frozen earth hums under Sleipnir's hooves. My half-brother is being ridden –

I jerk to a standstill. The music stops. The swirling dead fall silent.

My enemy is here.

29

THE MOTHER OF MONSTERS

NE-EYE HAS COME. Why? Why has he come? Why has he travelled down the gods' rainbow road to the long, sloping path the fateless walk between Midgard and Niflheim? To join our revels? Impossible.

The hall is in uproar. The dead smell the heat of the living; they sense the presence of the Lord of the Gods,

Father of the Slain. I've never heard such shrieking, such wailing, such terror. Winds gust. The candles splutter and go out.

I stagger to my throne.

Does he mean to kill me? He means to kill me.

And I also realise that I don't want to die.

I am frozen on my High Seat. I'm not a queen any more – I'm a terrified child. I can't fight him; the old wizard is too powerful for me. If I brought my hall crashing down on his head, he'd walk away and I'd be crushed.

And then he does something very strange.

One-Eye stands at the entrance, holding Sleipnir's reins and then *peeks* inside.

I sit very still. He surveys the hall overflowing and crammed with the dead, shields shimmering, gold decorating the benches. He looks – he looks afraid. And I don't know why.

He says nothing. Then he vanishes.

I hear his footsteps, heading for the eastern door,

leading Sleipnir. I am shaking.

He hasn't come for me. He has come to question the seeress, tear her from her grave and force secrets from her. That's One-Eye, always seeking to control the present and the future with his ripped knowledge of the past.

I won't let him leave me here. He can take me to Baldr.

I slide from my throne, abandoning my heavy furs, and haltingly make my way to the eastern door, cursing my legs, my stumbling gait. Never before have I so longed to be able to run. The dead scatter like scythed weeds, but I can only lurch slowly to the door. What are they saying? What am I missing?

I hear voices arguing and cursing one another before I can see anything through the choking vapour.

'I am unwilling to speak more!' shouts the pale spectre who was once my mother.

'You are no seeress,' I hear One-Eye bellow. 'You're a fool and the mother of monsters.'

I hear my mother's gloating voice. 'All the forces of darkness will gather at your doom,' she says, before sinking back into her grave.

One-Eye slumps at the mound, sleet swirling around him. His head is bowed, as if he is shouldering the nine worlds on his back.

'Free me,' I scream. 'What harm did I ever do you? What harm is foretold about me? None! Take me back with you!'

One-Eye appears not to notice me. I am far from his thoughts. Whatever knowledge of the future he has forced from my accursed mother, it is not what he wants to hear.

He swings up onto Sleipnir's back. Now I am begging and pleading, without pride.

I am an ant talking to a giant.

30

BOO HOO FOR YOU

OMETHING IS happening. My trembling kingdom shakes, as if my brother Fen is roaring and raging in his chains. Bones clatter to the ground. Jagged cracks tear open the walls. Benches slide and crash along the heaving floor while the chandeliers sway on their chains. The mead goat flees, bellowing.

Is it the end of the world? Has the doom of the gods crept up so quickly, without warning? Or is it just one of my brothers thrashing his tail?

And then again, another quake. And another. Thunderbolt upon thunderbolt. The shades moan and mutter, whining like wasps as they teem through my shuddering hall.

Something is happening. First Odin, full of woe, raises the seeress, and now this.

I question every new shade. Is the world ending? Why did Odin come? Have the giants attacked? Have my brothers escaped and avenged me? I can smell it, even here in my forsaken kingdom.

I, who have not felt impatience for aeons, suddenly cannot be still. I flit from my bed to my throne, and then back to my chamber, opening and closing my curtains till they moulder in my hands. I pace restlessly, as unsettled as any newly buried corpse.

Why can no one answer my queries? News travels so slowly between the worlds. Yet the slumbering wolf misses his prey.

I cannot wait here. I go to Gjoll. Modgud is full of questions about the feast, then stops when she sees my grim face.

Modgud knows nothing. I want to scream.

'Ask them,' I say. 'Forget their names – find out what cataclysm has happened.'

She does.

No one knows anything.

I join Modgud by Gjoll's bridge. I shove her aside, and pepper the dead with questions myself.

'Has the Axe Age come? Has winter strangled Midgard? Are there biting winds, ice, no summers in between?'

The dead shake their heads. 'It is always the Axe Age,' they moan, recoiling when they see me.

My shoulders are up to my ears. My black nails are bitten. I don't know what to do. I am shaking with rage.

And then through the sleet I see something small

darting down the Fog Road, weaving past the trudging corpses. It gesticulates frantically, whimpering and bellowing by turns.

Modgud leaps to her feet.

'I demand to see Hel!' shouts a gnobbly voice. Then the agitated shade of a dwarf oozes past, screeching as he struggles to reach me through the swarming wraiths.

'There's been a terrible mistake!' he wails.

Amazing. Even dead dwarfs have no manners.

'I'm dead before my time!' he screams. 'If only I hadn't gone to the funeral! I demand to go back where I belong!'

Oh gods, one of those. I yawn.

'Boo hoo for you. Now get out of here.'

The dwarf sets his hands on his hips – or where his hips would have been if he still had any.

'You don't know what's happened, do you?' he said.

'To you? I couldn't care less,' I said. 'Look around you, dwarf.'

'The great god Baldr is dead. Baldr, god of light, is dead.'

31
EARTHQUAKE

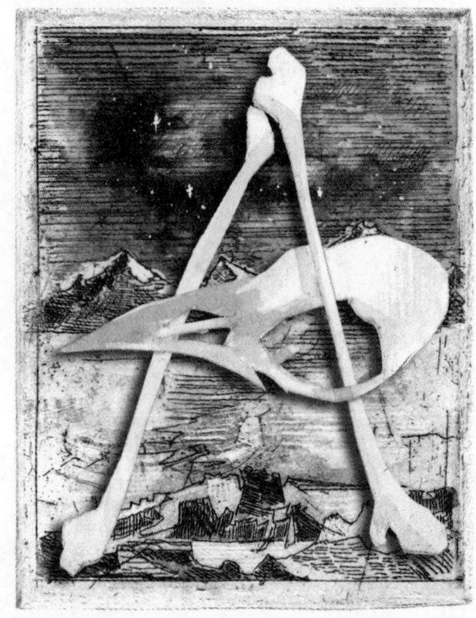

FROZEN HAND squeezes my throat. I can't breathe.

The dwarf rambles on but I can't hear him. There is a roaring in my head, like a howling hurricane. If I hadn't been seated, I would have collapsed. Modgud covers her mouth with her hands.

'What did you say?'

'I was at his funeral. I shouldn't be here. I have work

to do. I've left my forge –'

'Shut up. Who cares about you? How did Baldr die?' I whisper.

If in battle, he'll go to Valhall. They'd make a place for him, of course. But if not – he'd come here!! To me!!!

'It was an accident. His blind brother, Hod, killed him with a mistletoe dart. All things in the nine worlds but mistletoe had sworn an oath not to harm Baldr. So the gods were having fun hurling stones and weapons at Baldr, which left him unharmed, until the sharpened mistletoe pierced him. They say Loki put Hod up to it.'

I swallow. Then Baldr had not died in battle. He was coming here. To Hel. My head jerks forward. I think I might faint.

Modgud clutches my arm. I shake her off. Of course there were earthquakes. The death of a god is a cataclysm. No wonder One-Eye came to raise the seeress.

Baldr is dead. Baldr is dead. I don't think I have ever heard lovelier words.

'Tell me what happened.'

'Will you send me back?' asks the dwarf.

Idiot.

'I'll feed you to the dragon if you don't speak. He loves eating dwarfs.'

The dwarf puffs out his chest. The newly dead still retain much of their living spirit – it takes time for the self to fade.

'The gods couldn't launch Baldr's funeral ship, the greatest of all ships. They were weak with weeping, so they sent for a giantess to lend a hand. Hyrrokin came riding on her wolf bridled with vipers, and a bunch of us tagged along after her – I mean, how often do you get to go to the funeral of a god? Never! What a sight: Freyja in her cat chariot, and Frey with his golden boar, and the Valkyries, and rock giants and elves and –'

'I don't need a guest list,' I interrupt.

'Anyway, Hyrrokin gripped the ship's high prow and pulled it down into the heaving water, so hard that the rollers burst into flame and the nine worlds trembled and quaked as the boat crashed into the waves.

'And then four weeping gods lifted Baldr's shrouded body and placed it on the bed high in the boat, which was filled with treasures and the slaughtered body of his horse. Odin jumped into the boat, took off his arm ring and placed it on Baldr's chest.

'I was craning to see – I'm short – I wanted to watch the boat catch fire, and all those gods and giants were blocking my view. I hate tall people – they're so inconsiderate – so I ran closer to the water's edge, just minding my own business, pushing through the crowds, saying, 'Move, move, let me through,' and ran in front of Thor who was hallowing the blaze and chanting charms, and he stuck out his foot, tripped me, and then kicked me so hard out of the way that I landed on Baldr's burning ship. I burned to death!' he screams, stamping his foot. 'I died before my time. It's so unfair! I wasn't hurting anyone, I just –'

The dwarf drones on.

I close my eyes and see Baldr's funeral boat as it

drifted across the rippling sea, burning and crackling as the winds whipped the pyre and swept him on his journey here.

His journey to me.

'Flames scorched the water, then the cold finger of the underworld reached up, and the boat crumbled into ash. But with me in it!' wails the dwarf. 'Now I've said all I know. Will you send me back?'

'No,' I reply. 'Your days and deeds are finished. Leave me.'

Immediately his shade melts into the murk.

Baldr is coming. He'll be here at last. He'll be here any moment. I can't believe it. After all these centuries, so much heavy time, and he is coming to join me. Everyone wants him. Everyone loves him.

And now he is mine until the End of Days.

I must prepare. Baldr loves me. I know he does. He sees past my deformity and into my heart. He always did. Last time he saw me I was a stupefied, frightened, battle-shocked child. I may still look like one, but now I'm a queen. Oh my gods, what should I wear? My storeroom is packed with grave goods – I must put on something gorgeous. Necklaces! Bracelets. Rings. I must gleam in the murk, shine like no other in this raven-dark world. I will be laden with gold: my arms, my neck, my hair, my breasts. I will blaze like a burnished shield, bright as dragonfire.

I practically skip through the bleak valleys back to Eljudnir. I clap my hands, scattering the teeming shades. I must deck my death hall as well, strew the floor with fresh rushes, hang tapestries to cover the walls, make it beautiful for my beautiful Baldr. The servants are stunned. They've never seen me take any interest in my 'guests'. I shout for Slowpoke and Lazybones, which is pointless, pointless, as they have never and will never move with speed, but I call for them anyway, so desperate am I to be ready for my love; then I press-gang any of the dead with limbs to decorate the hall with gold, to shine my welcome, make my hall glorious with rich hangings.

For the first time in forever, I need to make haste.

I watch the benches being gilded with gold arm rings and I'm suddenly terrified he won't remember me. But he will, he will! Of course he will. I am ablaze with light, with happiness, with a joy I've only ever felt once before, when he whirled me in his arms.

32

WELCOME

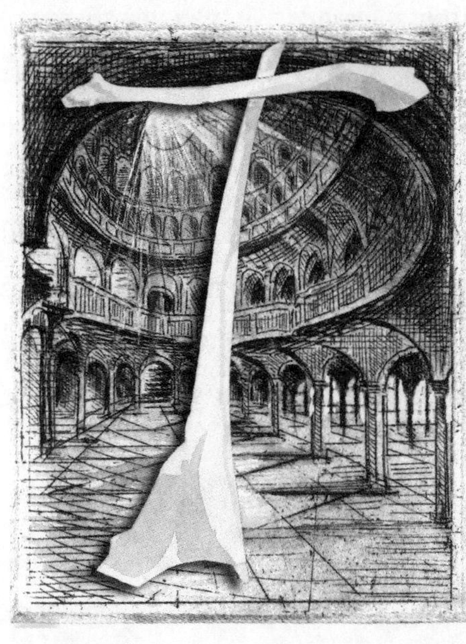

HE CARRION GATES are open. The stone hearths blaze with fire. The hall gleams gold and bronze, pockets of light in the smoky gloom. I blink in the unfamiliar glow. Gold and silver bowls fill the tables; jewelled drinking horns rest in their holders. If the place stinks, I can't smell the death reek any more. My Baldr won't care. I am dressed like a queen. I can't stop stroking my robes – how smooth my petticoat of silky pleated linen feels. My overdress is heavily embroidered; a pair of oval brooches, laden and twisted with silver, shine on my shoulders. My bright gold necklace, the tribute of a Midgard queen, hangs heavy on my neck. How did she wear this, I wonder. It weighs so much I have to lean back so as not to tip forward. My blue fur cape drapes over my throne and trails along the floor. It's all for show – I don't feel the cold – but it is so magnificent I could not leave it off. What joy I had choosing what to wear! The night I spent in my treasure room trying on this robe and that, flinging rejects to the floor – too mouldy, too large, too small – unable to choose.

The hall stirs. He's coming! I smooth my hair, bite my lips, try to breathe.

Bells should be ringing, not just the howls of Garm, frightened and cowed by the golden one's approach. Why didn't I think of that? Or dragged out one of those musicians, ordered him to sing. Baldr likes poetry, music. Most people do except me . . . How could I have forgotten? We'll have stories and music every night if that's his wish. I don't have to listen; I can just look at him.

Hurry, my love! Why are you so slow? I never dreamed this night could come – how can a god die? – and yet it has happened. Baldr is coming here. The Fates have treated me cruelly, and yet today their countenances smile upon me.

The wall sconces dangle with jewels. I too can make a kingdom glow. I'm on my black throne, in the High Seat of my gem-decked hall, bright rings and precious armbands cover the benches. The High Seat beside me, the place of honour, carved with runes, is decorated and ready. We will rule this world together. The place throngs with rustling shades, eager to see the great one, the first of the gods ever to die.

There is a hush, and bright Baldr stands in the doorway. Light pours off his ghostly body, illuminating my hall like a shooting star. What's killed him has left no mark. I'm timid. I can't help it – I don't feel like a queen; I feel like a little girl. Welcome, my darling! Welcome! I've never loved anyone before; no one has ever loved me. I don't know whether to scream or faint.

I watch as he walks slowly towards me, rippling through the hall, lighting the way through the shadows with his beauty, hesitating, uncertain, bewildered, just like they all are, the new arrivals. He is no different, my lovely one, and my heart melts at his awkwardness. Then he sees me and – smiles his wonderful smile. He is more glorious, more radiant, than I remember. I don't want to sit up here like some boulder, I want to run to him, sobbing, but . . . I look so much better seated. So much more – normal. If I staggered to him, I'd just fall over. What a bad beginning that would be. He doesn't want a cripple. Let me awe him with my power, and then put him at ease with my kindness, my quick wit. I won't rush. I have promised myself I won't rush.

So. I stay put. My throat is dry. I'm the queen . . . I'm the queen. The shining mead awaits in the cauldron. I have only to command the shield be lifted and the drink will be served to him in goblets of silver filigree. How grateful I am for all the riches the sons and daughters of Midgard shove in the grave mounds of their dead.

'Hel,' he says. And he tries to smile again. 'You look all grown up.'

I am so overcome I can't say anything.

'I never thought we'd meet here.' His voice. Honey and birdsong. I lean towards him like a sun-seeking flower. I have so much to say. I'm just going to tell him straight out how much I love him, that I've waited for him, what he means to me, that this is a new beginning, that the Fates meant this, for him, for me, for us.

'Baldr,' I begin.

I gaze at him, my love-longing written on my face. He looks startled, his timeless eyes widening, then he flinches.

I feel blood pounding in my head. I've given myself away too soon. He needs time to adjust.

But I can recover. There's no rush. I start again.

'Baldr. Welcome. I wish –'

I wish what? That we were meeting somewhere else? Definitely. That he was still alive? No.

'Well, you understand,' I fumble.

He nods, courtly, calm again.

I try to smile. Can he see my heart beating? I hold out a horn of mead.

'Baldr,' I begin again, 'Do you remember when –'

There's a stirring in the hall. The skull-guests flutter. Who's here? Who dares enter?

It's *her*. She's followed him, hurled herself into his burning ship. She stands at my entrance. And I cannot slam the gates to bar her.

I freeze, my words rotting and turning to ash in my mouth.

Baldr turns and runs.

He grabs Nanna in his arms while she weeps and clutches his neck and buries her face in his shoulder.

I am forgotten. I was never remembered. My body feels hacked by a hundred axes. My hopes smash like spear-shattered ice. The horn drops and spills.

I scream. The rain-damp hall shudders. Baldr ran to his wife, his beautiful wife. They have their story, and I am not in it.

Hel the Awful.

Hel the Ugly.

Hel who will never, ever, win Baldr.

So now you know.

I howl. Whatever I do, it will never be enough. However much love I have for him, he will never feel it for me. It wouldn't matter if I fell over or stayed still. How I looked. What I said. If I scowled or if I smiled. Whether I wore gold or bronze. Whether I had two legs or twenty. I am no more to him than the clustering shades jamming my hall and the corpses pouring through the door to glimpse him.

What sustained me here in Hel, what kept me going, was him. I drank words of poetry. I allowed myself to dream.

I was a fool.

Go on, laugh at me. I dare you.

My slow servants move towards me. I dig my nails into my arm, to shut myself up. I am Queen of the Dead. I'm a goddess. Everyone fears me. I must control myself, I must –

I continue crying, but silently now. Do not pity me. This is the last time I will ever cry. The restless shades stir, uneasy. Vapour drips down the walls, staining my foolish tapestries. The stench of my hall reaches my nostrils. Garm howls. Go on, Garm, good dog, always a comfort. Howl away.

I swallow, and speak. My mouth tastes of metal.

'You will sit beside me,' I say.

Baldr obeys. He walks up the slimy stone steps towards the empty throne. Nanna follows him.

'Not her. Just you.'

Instantly Nanna fades off into the darkness where the shades huddle on benches. I'm queen. She has to obey. There's solace in that.

How I hate her.

Baldr sits beside me. He doesn't look at me, and I don't look at him. My heart is black ice. I feel the rot in my legs creep up my body until I am more dead than alive.

And there we sit, in silence. I struggle to control myself. I can stop my voice. I can't stop my tears. They flow like Gjoll, an endless stream down my face.

I am rain-drenched, sleet-cold.

I wanted him to want me. I wanted his face to fill with joy when he saw me, not flash with light because he has seen Nanna. I wanted him to make my eye the first he seeks to catch. I wanted to be the one he shared his life and death with.

I wanted him to want me.

That's over.

33
THE WORLD WEEPS

KNOW THE GODS will try to get Baldr back. They won't let me keep him. They'll offer me a ransom to let him ride home to Asgard. They'll beg and plead and threaten, and I must decide what to do.

Because if I can't have Baldr no one can.

I sit on my throne, the stone-faced god beside me, his body twitching with revulsion, and I wonder who they'll send down on their wooing mission. His mother Frigg, weeping and wailing? A mother's greasy tears mean nothing to me. I'd enjoy laughing at her. They'll have to do better than that. One-Eye? Nah, he likes others to do his dirty work. Dear old Dad is unlikely, since he caused Baldr's death in the first place. On the other hand, maybe he'll come to make amends. Isn't that his style? Make a mess, then charm his way out? What a pleasure that would be, spitting in his face.

Already I can hear Gjoll's bridge thundering under Sleipnir's hooves. I wonder if Modgud will let whoever is coming pass over. After all this time, all that guarding, finally she gets to spring into action.

Well, I'm not going to make it easy for what's-his-face. My Hel gates are locked and barred. My fortress walls should keep out anyone alive, even a god: I built my ramparts high and strong for this moment.

Garm barks, an eerie echoing howl. I feel living breath whoosh through our gloom. The mystery god is approaching. I am cold, detached, as if I am observing a scene, not about to take part in it. I want to see Baldr's face when I raise his hopes, and then dash them. I am fire and ice: I am nothing now except hissing hate.

He is making so much noise, Baldr's would-be rescuer. I really, really hope it's not Loki. He must be half dead (ha ha) after such a long ride to get here. The shadows tremble around me – the dead don't like their slumber disturbed and recently it's been one cataclysm after the other. You'd think they'd enjoy a bit of change, a little variety, something to break up an eternity of deadness, but no: eventually the dead seem to like being dead. How they moan if anyone troubles their grave mound. Variety isn't the spice of death.

In my mind, I see my half-brother prancing across Gjoll's gold-thatched bridge as the icy waters of the final river churn beneath it. I hear the thrumming of my brother's eight hooves. Niflheim resounds with their clatter. And now the mad galloping gets closer. Time to move. I leave Baldr the Fair, immobile on his High Seat, stony and hateful, and I creep into my chamber, pull the hangings across and sink into my musty bed.

Whoever has come can wait. This is my party.

There's a whistling sound, then I hear the booming thud of Sleipnir landing hard, hooves smashing rocks. Odin's horse, my half-brother, has jumped my gate. He's *inside* my stronghold, and now there's no way I can stop him.

There is a brisk *clump-clump clump-clump clump-clump clump-clump*, which only stops outside Eljudnir's open door. The dead shift and whimper, flapping like drowning insects.

I peek through the curtains.

A god appears in the doorway of my hall. Like Baldr, and yet not like Baldr. I recognise Hermod, One-Eye's son, Baldr's brother.

This is my *kingdom*, I remind myself. *These beings have done all the hurt they can do you. They are far from Asgard now.*

I keep Hermod waiting all night. I stay in my bed. It feels good to lie there and drift, to empty my mind.

Finally, when I am as ready as I would ever be, I draw back the black hangings and slowly creep towards Hermod. I still don't know what I will say, what I will decide. The fateless around me, decomposing bone-bags, are in tumult. Their eyes – those who still have eyes – are fixed on Hermod, sitting by the door. I feel him trembling. The Kingdom of the Dead dismays even immortals. Hermod is staring straight at Baldr; if he sees me enter he makes no sign. But I sense him watching me.

I ignore him, creep towards my throne. My dragging legs are the only sound echoing around this oozing death cavern. Baldr is still sitting in the High Seat silent, beautiful. His pale face shines like polished marble. Even now, my heart lurches when I see him. I crush it like a fig.

Hermod prostrates himself before me. Imagine that. One of the gods bowing before me, stretched out on my filthy floor.

'Why have you come to Hel?' I say. I want to hear him beg and plead.

I let Hermod boo hoo about how much the gods missed Baldr, how empty and desolate Asgard is without him – ha! That makes me happy! – and then he asks me – I knew it – if I will let Baldr ride home with him.

I sit in silence, looking down at the pleading god. I'm good at silence. I feel the world holding its breath, waiting for my decision. Outside my gates I hear my brother stomping his hooves, his hot, living breath pouring out of his mouth into the fetid murk. He whickers and I feel his fear.

'And where were you when Odin kidnapped me and hurled me here?' I ask. I speak slowly. My lips are unaccustomed to speech now; my tongue feels thick in my mouth.

'The All-Father decides, and we obey,' says Hermod.

I know that, of course I know that. I just want to enjoy my moment of power. Can you blame me?

'Yet now you want something from me.'

Hermod bows his head.

'The gods are weeping for Baldr. The world is

weeping for Baldr, the much-loved.'

Much loved. He knows nothing about much-loved, I think. I control my face, keep it grim and fierce. I don't have love, but I have pride. The world loves him more than I did? I bristle. But I hold my face steady. If I betray myself, those hateful skalds and bards and poets will compose songs mocking me, and that I could not bear. 'Death be not proud?' I'll be as proud as I like.

'I'm not so sure that Baldr is so loved as you say. Why don't we put it to the test?'

Hermod's face lights up. He is hardly daring to hope, yet I have not said no.

'Anything,' says Hermod.

'If all things in the world, living and dead, weep for Baldr, then let him return with you to Asgard. But if even one thing does not weep, if even one creature speaks against him, then Baldr remains here, with me.'

I can see Hermod struggling to control his face. He looks at Baldr, who suddenly flashes a smile. Baldr is confident that everyone and everything loves him. What must that feel like, to know that you are so beloved? I've never been loved and I cannot imagine it. I feel such a strong gush of hate that I am chilled.

Then Baldr rises up and goes to his brother. He hands him a beautiful arm ring, heavy with gold. 'Give this to our father, to remember me,' he says.

I should have claimed that ring as tribute, I think.

Nanna, too, appears from the shades, holding a linen smock and other gifts. They walk with Hermod the desolate length of my hall, back to the door. I turn away, return to my diseased bed and pull the curtains. I don't want to see Baldr happy in another's company. The sight stabs my heart.

Will the world weep Baldr out of Hel? Really? Every bird? Every tree? Every snake and every stone? Fire, and iron, silver and gold, all crying for him?

Let the world and everything in it weep Baldr out of Hel and away from me.

Because I won't let him go otherwise.

34

LET HEL HOLD WHAT SHE HAS

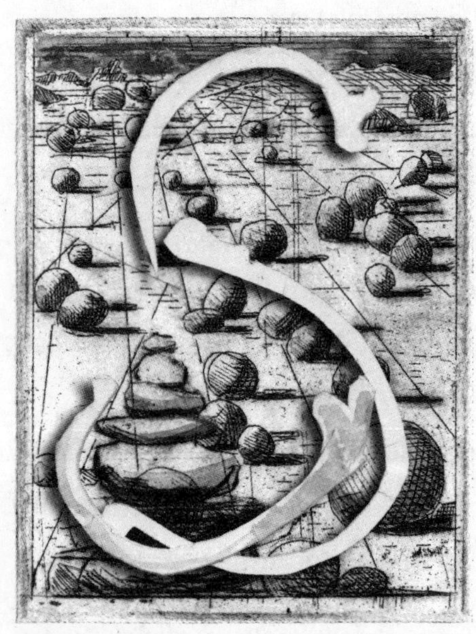

SO WAS I RIGHT OR was I right?

The gods scoured the Nine Worlds, and the din of weeping reached even me.

Yet no god returned, gleeful and rejoicing, to escort Baldr back to life.

One giantess, Thokk, alone in her cave, refused to mourn. Her harsh words reverberated through the worlds, repeated and repeated, and finally drifted down to me.

Thokk will weep
waterless tears
over Baldr's funeral pyre.
Living or dead,
I loved not One-Eye's son;
Let Hel hold what she has.

I smiled when I heard that, the last I would ever smile, and for nights I could not hide my glee. How I wished I could fling gold rings at that marvellous creature, lavish her with swords and shields and axes inlaid with ivory. I had my vengeance on One-Eye. How he wanted his bonny boy back.

But mine was the victory. Baldr stayed with me. What a triumph. That's one in the eye for the mortal gods. And even if Baldr does not love me, will never love me, at least the gods won't have him either. A bitter win. He is here in body, but his mind, spirit, heart are elsewhere.

Let Hel hold what she has.

And what do I have?

Before Baldr came, I lived through ghostly dreams of him. Dreams of joy, dreams of happiness, dreams of love.

That's over.

So how do I continue with my life?

My Death Hall is too cheerful. The freezing mists, the toxic dead, are far too welcoming now.

I think about moving.

I could make my tomb-home near the dragon, in the lowest, darkest pit of Niflheim, where corpses wade through turbid streams into the serpent's jaws. I would admit only murderers and perjurers, baleful company in my bleakness. My doors would face north and I would lie in sickness and disease, the only sound the dragon's crunching jaws as he gnaws on corpses. I would lace my roof with vipers.

I have no will to move from my bed. I have not moved for nights now.

I focus my mind, and snakes burst from the walls and burrow themselves into the rafters. I hate snakes, so I wattle my roof with them. Serpents hissing and spitting and twisting, their heads blowing venom, with poison dripping down the walls from the smoke holes.

That's better.

Now for my skull-guests.

No more ale will be brewed. I won't serve mead any more – the dead can have horns full of piss if they want to drink.

No more sagas told. I will shut up the storytellers, stop their mouths. There will be no more noise.

I will live in silence.

Just so we're clear. Just so you know. No one can die out of Hel, not even Baldr. *You* certainly can't be wept out of the Underworld.

So all that yowling from your kin achieves nothing.

In fact, the din of weeping makes me crazy.

'Quiet!' I howl.

Their lamentations circle and bind me into a coffin.

And then their mourning cries join the dead who whirl around me in a cacophony of shrieking moans.

The din of yakking voices is like a hammer cracking open my head.

'BE QUIET, ALL OF YOU!' I roar. 'I decree, no one can speak unless spoken to.'

And, just like that, silence descends in my hall.

I see their mouths opening, and their cracked teeth, and they are screaming into the void.

Silence.

And still they move their green mouths, and wave their bony fingers, and open their lipless skulls to form angry words and – nothing comes out.

The quiet of my grave hall is total.

The burning inside me eases.

Suddenly I can breathe again. The pounding in my head stops.

The relief is indescribable.

I don't have to hear any more whining and wailing and moaning and groaning.

Why hadn't I done this before?

I sit up and pull my mucky bedhangings closed.

I will lie and rot on my bed and I will hate for one long everlasting winter's night without end.

I smell like festering regrets and carrion too rank for ravens. I won't be bottling my scent *I STINK* any time soon.

I scream silently, for eternity.

I lie behind foul curtains on my damp bed. A mildewed blanket is pulled up to my waist. My servant Lazybones spends one night bringing me a glass of wine, so slowly that I barely see her move, then another night removing the empty goblet. I listen to the rustling of the dead as they prowl my hall, hear the hissing snakes, watch poison dribble down my walls.

Oh, how could I forget – I still name things. My gold plate I've renamed Hunger – it is never filled. My knife I call Starving. It cuts nothing. I've spent longest naming my bed hangings. Right now they're called Shining Harm.

I called them Rickets for a millenia, then I fancied a change. I might try Glimmering Misfortune next.

I am alone and I am unloved. Loneliness gnaws my core like a cancer.

Enough of these thoughts. Thinking them brings me no peace.

My bed didn't start out putrid. My bed hangings weren't always threadbare. My plate wasn't always empty. But after Baldr – no, I've sworn not to think about him, I have cut him out of my heart along with hope. I lie still in the gloom, while everything moulders around me. Grief lies beside me, swelling the blanket.

All I have now is revenge. That's what I wake to, that's what I sleep to. My revenge on the gods.

PART 4
Shining Harm

35
VISITORS

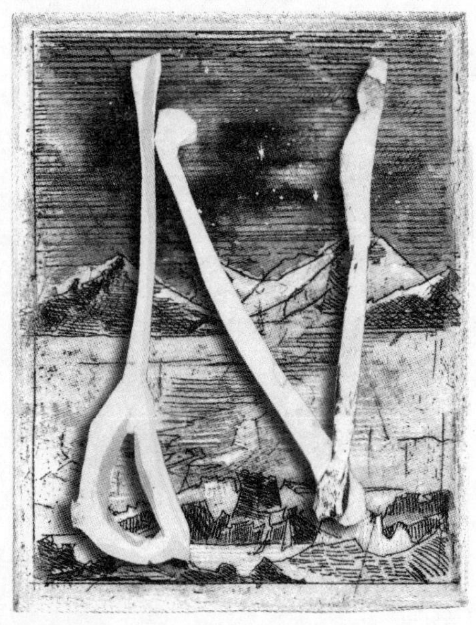

IGHTS PASS. WEEKS. Years. Centuries. I've no idea. Time has no measure here. I just want to lie and decay, and the world won't leave me alone. What's that Viking saying? You wait forever for a chariot, and then three turn up at once.

I am inert on Sickbed. (Where else would I be?) My face to the wall. My thoughts black as tar. Listening to the *drip drip drip* of snake venom dribbling down the walls.

I hear the bed curtains part. They're brittle now; they rip and crumble. I don't move. Not sure I can move any more, even if I wanted to.

'Hel?'

It's Modgud. It has been aeons since I've seen her, aeons since I've heard another voice. Strange, I'd forgotten all about her.

'What's happened?' she whispers. 'Why are you just – lying here? Why are there snakes everywhere?'

I'm not sure I even remember how to speak.

'Leave me alone,' I say. My voice is hoarse. My mouth tastes of sand.

'You don't have to be like this,' says Modgud.

'Go away.'

'We could throw stones into Gjoll again,' says Modgud. 'I've learned how to make them skip – I can show you.'

I don't reply.

She tries again.

'You should see the grave-wagon of stuff that just

came over the bridge. *Very* generous kin.'

Does the stupid giant really think a few trinkets can cheer me?

'You left the bridge,' I say. 'It's forbidden.'

Modgud takes a step back. 'A god is coming,' she says. 'I came to warn you.'

I open my heavy eyelids.

What is this, Asgard by the swamp?

'Why didn't you stop him?' I hiss. 'You're supposed to guard the bridge, not offer guided tours. You stupid troll.'

Why can't everyone just leave me alone? I don't care about anything. I want to die.

'Hel,' she begins. 'Please –'

'Get back to the bridge,' I say.

Modgud's face bleaches whiter. She turns and leaves.

And then my father swaggers in.

36

I'VE MISSED YOU

OKI SWAGGERS IN as though we'd just said farewell a few nights ago.

He looks the same. Handsome. Jaunty. Treacherous with his viper eyes of red and green.

'Hello, daughter. Aren't you looking well,' he says, leering at me through my slimy curtains. His eyes glitter. Then he pushes through the drapes, stands over me and twists his face into a smile.

I don't even bother to raise my head. I never thought I would see him again.

'Leave me alone,' I say. I close my eyes.

'Is that any way to greet your dad?' he said. 'Your loving dad?'

I'll have to handle this myself.

'Are you dead? Your days and deeds finished? Please say yes.'

Dad grins his wolf smile. 'Not yet.'

'Then why are you here?'

'Can't a father visit his daughter without having a motive?' he says. 'I've missed you.'

'You seem to have managed fine without me,' I reply.

'That's more than I can say for you, daughter,' he says. 'Look at the state of this place. You're a queen . . . I wouldn't kennel a dog here.' He wrinkles his nose.

What do I care what he thinks of my décor?

'Go to the trolls,' I say.

'And after I've travelled all this way . . .' he says. 'You

surprise me, Hel. Especially when I come bearing gifts.'

Gifts?

Despite myself I slowly open my eyes. I have a weakness for gifts. Maybe I believe if I gather enough goods I will feel less empty.

'Trust me, you'll like it,' he says, holding out an intricately carved wooden *eski*. He flips open the lid.

Inside the box is a single brown nut.

I stare at him. He is mocking me. Why? Loki usually picks more challenging victims to tease.

'Well?' Dad keeps his voice level, but I can feel his excitement. He wants something from me. I am sure of it. My father has come to ask a favour.

As if I'd grant him anything.

'You've come to the world of the dead to bring me a nut,' I say. 'What kind of stupid trick is this?'

Dad snorts. 'You're not the only one who hates the gods, Hel,' he says. 'This is the goddess Idunn.'

'Who?' I ask. There are so many gods it is hard to keep track. Not that I want to, anyway. I am unlikely to be invited to join the children's table at any Asgard family gatherings any time soon.

'Hel, you're a stinking sow,' says Loki. 'Idunn!'

I don't know why he thought shouting her name would make any difference.

'Idunn, the Goddess of Youth, the keeper of the gods' immortality. Her golden apples keep the gods young. Without her . . .' He drew his finger across his neck. 'The gods are dying. Every last one of them. Odin included.' He beams. 'Then flickering flames will devour their halls, and even their names will vanish from the world.'

I never move in haste. In fact, I rarely even twitch. But at this I jolt upright.

In all my thoughts of vengeance, nothing so immense, so earth-shattering, had ever occurred to me.

My banishment would end. My enemies would be defeated. Not just defeated, but wiped from the worlds. I would be avenged! A fierce joy galvanises me. The first glimmer of joy I've felt since Baldr – I brush aside the sliver of ice his name always shoots through me.

Keeping Baldr here was a small revenge. Killing all the gods – this was a vengeance undreamt of.

I sit there silently, my face blank as an empty mead horn.

What, you think I jumped up and covered Loki with kisses and thanked him for devising the most perfect retribution on the evildoers who flung me here? Have you learned nothing? Loki can *never* be trusted. He is called Loki the Trickster for good reason.

He reads my mind.

'I'm a very good liar, but everything I'm telling you now is true,' he says.

My fingers tighten around my blanket and twist through the holes. The only sound is the snakes hissing in the roof, and the rustling of the raven food in the poisonous hall beyond my curtains.

'Well? Isn't this the revenge you've been longing for?' he asks.

'Prove it,' I say.

Dad grins his wolfish grin.

'Oh ye of little faith,' he says. He holds the nut between

his slender ivory hands and murmurs runes over it.

I brace myself. Has he brought Fen here? Or one of his hag daughters? Which monster will appear?

A trembling goddess stands before me, beautiful, glowing, clutching a basket of golden apples. The apples of immortality. She gags at her first breath of the fetid air.

'Let me go,' she whispers. 'I belong in Asgard. I need to get back to –'

Dad speaks the runes again and instantly she shrivels back into a nut.

Slowly, I lean forward.

'How did you kidnap . . . No, I don't want to know,' I say. 'What's in it for you?'

His face twists for a moment.

But his answer surprises me.

'I've been a bad boy . . . Let's just say the gods want to tie me to a rock and drip snake poison on my face till the End of Days and, frankly, I'd rather not have that fate. I just want to hide out here until the happy day of doom,' he says. 'It won't be long.'

Why am I always the last to hear good news?

'What have you done?'

He waves his hands. 'Oh, you know, bit of this, bit of that, bit of name calling at a feast – a few curses … Possibly a few secrets yelled out –'

No mention of Baldr. He hopes I don't know.

'Give me the *eski*,' I say. 'I'll hide it. No one will touch it.'

'I don't think that's wise,' says my father. 'I should keep –'

'I don't give a troll's fart what you think,' I say. 'I'm queen. This is my kingdom. If I let you stay, you'll obey me.'

Loki smiles and bows his head. Then he hands me the *eski*.

'Of course, Hel, whatever you say. You're the boss.'

Too right I am. I grip the precious box. It contains every drop of vengeance, all my blighted hopes, all my ruined dreams. Fierce happiness hurtles through my shattered body. Repay laughter with laughter. Gifts with gifts. And betrayal with treachery. The gods would pay dearly for what they'd done to me. Although luck has never been with me, tonight, luck swaddles me in her slippery arms.

'Find yourself a cave,' I tell him. 'I don't want you near me.'

So long as he keeps away, I don't care where he hides.

Loki smirks as if I have just offered him a chest of gleaming gold.

'Daughter,' he says. 'You honour me with your hospitality.'

Should I mention my mother? Give him her address? First grave mound on the left?

Nah.

I put the *eski* under my bed, lie back on my damp pillow and close my eyes.

All I have to do is wait. Wait in Hel for the mortal gods to fade away and die. I am happy to wait. Like the dead, my patience is boundless.

I could have waited forever.

And then . . .

And then Freya came.

And that changed everything.

37
FREYA

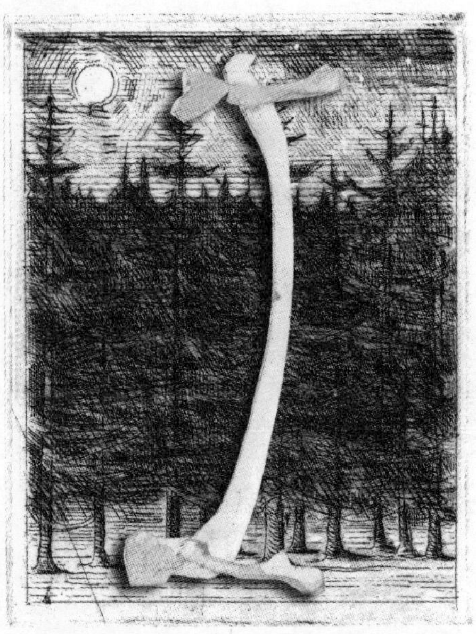

SMELLED HER FIRST.

I smelled the rich overpowering whiff of life. So did the restless corpses, agitated that flesh was coming. Garm barked madly.

Bit late, I thought, *you useless wolf.*

She came, disguised as a falcon, flying down inside Hekla, the volcano which is one of Hel's, shall we say, lesser-used entrances. I felt the whoosh of her wings, heard the flapping falling, the great *thunk* of her landing. I thought, *Oh gods, here we go again*. Another *shaman's spirit taking on a bird shape to try to wrench some dead soul from me*.

Then I heard her footsteps thudding across Modgud's echoing bridge, and I realised that this was no shaman's spirit but a mortal.

An actual mortal. The first and only living mortal ever to come here. A living, breathing person. Who was she? Who had sent her? I did not know what to think. How had the pulse managed it? Clearly she had unusual powers.

So for which corpse was the mortal going to beg and plead? I didn't care: the answer would of course be no. She wouldn't be returning to Midgard anyway.

I heard her clatter across my threshold like a bear sniffing fish. This mortal was either very brave or very stupid. I sent Lazybones to bring her to me. At the speed that old woman moves, the driftwood was in for a long wait.

As I lay hidden in my chamber, I heard voices. The tones grated on my ears, so long accustomed to silence. The mortal must have spoken to the corpses, and, boy, were they taking advantage. Snippets of conversation drifted to me.

I heard her pleading to know where she could find me.

Let her wait.

Let her enjoy her last moments of life.

38

DRESSED FOR THE TOMB

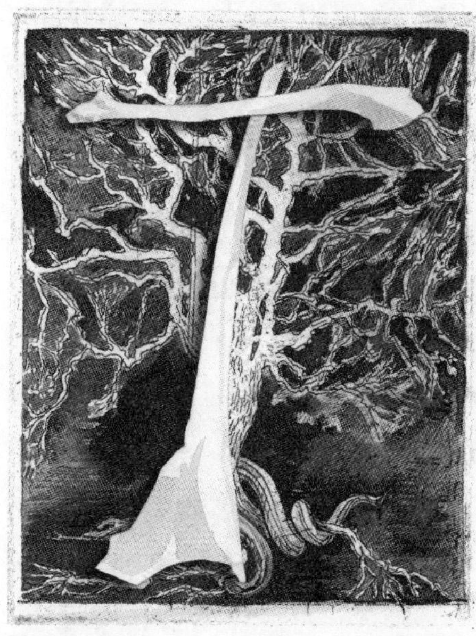

HE MORTAL STOOD outside my bed hangings. I heard her loud breaths, felt her fear. She stood there, still, uncertain, until I put my hand through the curtains and beckoned her in. I wanted to get this over with.

I lay there, eyes closed. The odour of her living body repelled me. Finally, she spoke.

'I'm looking for Hel,' she said. 'I need to speak to her urgently.'

Yeah well, the time-trapped are always in a rush. And what arrogance for driftwood to say it needed to speak to me.

'Excuse me,' she spoke again, 'I need to see Hel.'

Her voice was light, insistent. The creature was young. Very young. What madness possessed her to come here? How had she survived the journey?

Whoever she was, she didn't recognise me. The mortal is face to face with Death, and doesn't know it.

I opened my eyes.

'I heard you the first time.'

The girl's face went white with shock.

I stared at her battered, bruised cheeks, her mottled-ivory arms and hands, at the ivory creeping up to her throat, her filthy frosty clothes and scratched legs. Her hot breath.

This was the first living mortal I'd ever seen. The noise she'd made entering my hall made me imagine she was troll-sized. Yet she was very small, puny even. *One-Eye had nothing to be proud of if this was his best attempt at creation*, I thought. Her age? I'm hopeless at guessing ages – not really a skill I need, is it? – but I didn't think she was much more than a child. Like me, in fact. I had a sudden sense that if I'd been mortal and able-limbed, I could have been her. I pushed this thought away, as it served nothing.

'Why are you here before your time?' I asked.

The girl nervously ran her fingers through her curly hair, tugging it. She began to babble. The dying Odin had sent her (I trembled just hearing his hateful name), blah blah blah, she was trying to rescue Idunn. She'd turn into ivory and be frozen forever if she didn't succeed. Loki had . . .

I might have guessed the wolf's father was the reason for her coming.

So she wasn't here to whine for her mama.

That made a change.

I watched her shivering in the cold, wrapping her arms around herself. She wasn't dressed for the tomb.

'I know Loki is here somewhere,' she said. 'He stole Idunn. I must find her and bring her back to Asgard. The gods are dying. The world is dying. I am dying.'

I smiled inside. If only I could make the world die faster.

But while she spoke a memory stirred in the back of my mind that I couldn't quite grasp, something someone had told me long ago . . .

Then I remembered. The seeress. She'd warned me a mortal hero would come. That the hero would somehow affect me, affect the End of Days.

This little . . . *girl* couldn't be that hero. How was that possible? An ugly mortal girl recklessly named after the goddess Freyja but nothing like her?

And yet Odin had sent this child. Obviously senility had affected his judgement . . . and his eyesight.

I cursed the seeress for telling me too little.

The girl held out her ivory arms. Clearly she was under some kind of curse. The Old Wizard, most likely. Join the party, mortal.

'Help me,' she said.

Help her? I'd sooner chop off my hand. I sat up a little and the blanket slipped, revealing my oozing legs. I saw her face: revolted and horrified, her eyes sliding away from mine as I covered my body again.

'Not so pretty, am I?' I said.

That shut her up.

You want your mother back? Tough. Your husband? Too bad. Your friend, your granny, your child? Yah boo sucks to you. Nothing doing.

But Idunn? She wanted *Idunn?* Did the mortal have *any* idea what she was asking? The presumption, the arrogance, was breathtaking. I'll send the driftwood to Nidhogg and end this now, I thought, before the begging and pleading starts.

But, as I moved, the bed curtains parted and Loki sauntered in. He made himself comfortable at the end of my bed, as if I were his poorly guest and he was checking to see how I was.

The girl's face went purple with anger. She looked as if she'd like to rip his eyes out.

I had ordered him to keep away from me, and here he was entering my chamber at will.

How dare he disobey?

'Who said you could come into my bed closet?' My voice was ice.

Loki laughed. 'I go where I please.'

'Not here you don't,' I said. 'Hel is *my* kingdom. You're here because I allow it.'

Dad's viper eyes flickered.

The mortal began to scream at him.

'Where is Idunn? Give her back to me!'

'Who's the pulse?' he said, jerking his thumb at the shivering girl.

'You know perfectly well who she is and why she's here,' I said.

Loki pretended he'd heard nothing.

'I'll show her out,' he said, then looked at Freya. 'You don't belong here.'

'*You* get out,' I ordered. 'Leave us alone. I don't often get to speak to someone with skin on their bones.' I would decide what happened to the mortal, not him.

'Where is Idunn?' screeched the girl. She was so fixed on her mission she didn't even notice her reprieve.

'Safe,' said Loki.

'Everyone is dying because of you,' said the mortal.

'Good,' said Dad. She shrank from him, trying not to touch the curtains, trying not to touch my bed.

'I know what my fate holds,' he said. 'A man's fate should be hidden, but I know mine. One day the gods will catch me, bind me to three sharp stones with the guts of my own son, and a snake will drip poison on my face until the End of Days. Drip. Drip. Drip. Who wouldn't do whatever they had to do, to avoid such a fate?'

No wonder he'd stolen Idunn. Had to hand it to Dad, he always knew how to justify himself.

'Bring Idunn back to Asgard,' the girl said. 'The gods will be grateful.'

'No chance,' said Loki.

My mind began to wander as they argued, away from their story. I kept seeing my father shackled and I longed to make this happen.

'All the gods will be dead soon,' Loki continued. 'Then I'll return to Asgard and thwart my fate. I'm writing a new ending. No being chained to a rock with poison dripping on my face. Just me. One god. One all-powerful, immortal god.'

A new ending. I tucked the phrase away in my word hoard, to consider later. I'm not stupid. When the gods died, Dad's take-over plans wouldn't include me. Most likely he'd keep me trapped here.

'I hate the gods,' I said. 'That doesn't mean I want *you* ruling, Dad. Now leave us alone and get out of my hall.'

My father bowed. 'Whatever you say, Queen of the Dead,' he said. He edged round the bed and went to the chamber's entrance. Then he turned. 'What in the name of the accursed gods do you think you're doing, you ugly little troll?' he hissed at me. His red and green eyes glared.

'I rule here, Father.'

'Why not keep the mortal if you like her so much?' I laughed.

'I can wait. Let her have her brief moment of light and warmth. Everyone ends up here in the end.' Then I turned over and faced the wall.

Loki slipped out. I knew he'd be waiting nearby, watching and waiting to strike.

I turned back and looked at the little girl. I'd used her against Dad: now he was gone, her usefulness to me was over.

'Will you help me?' asked Freya.

I paused for a long time. The mortal never took her pleading eyes off my face.

'How'd you like to spend eternity lying in a sickbed hung with curtains called Glimmering Misfortune, and be waited on by two servants called Slowpoke and Lazybones who move so slowly that they might as well be dead again because no one would notice?' I said, raising my creaking body to sit up. 'I never get out, I have no friends – in fact, everyone hates me. I have to spend my time with gangrenous, rotting raven food. I just lie here all day waiting for a cup of wine, then all night waiting for it to be removed.'

The girl sat there, listening. Her face in the shadowy candlelight was masked.

'I'm glad the gods are dying. They kidnapped me when I was a child, then Odin took one look at me and hurled me here, into this dark world below the worlds. "You'll like it," he said. "You'll be queen down there." Well, I don't like it. Not at all. So, no, I won't help you. Now go away.'

39

I'M A MONSTER

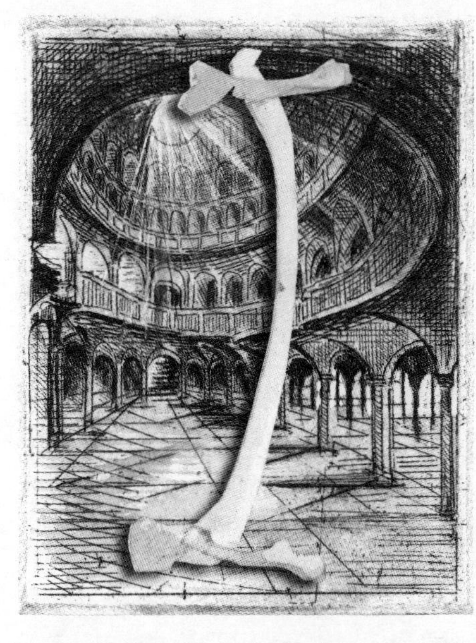

LAY BACK AND closed my eyes. I felt her staring at me, at my legs, so I yanked the curtains closed, shutting her out.

Bye-bye, hero. In the distance, I could hear Garm howling. What, he's only just realised there's an intruder around? Stupid dog.

My serving woman, Ganglot, waited silently by the threshold. Slowly she started to point to the exit.

And then, suddenly, I didn't want Freya to leave. I felt so lonely I didn't think I could bear it.

Maybe I'd keep her just a little bit longer.

'Wait,' I said, poking my hand through the tattered bed curtains.

Freya froze.

I beckoned to her again. I suddenly saw my cracked, curved nails, more like a wolf's than a god's.

I curled up my hand.

'Stay for a moment,' I said. 'Nice to look at someone who's still got skin on their face. Makes a change.'

Freya hesitated. Then, carefully, she sat on the edge of my bed. A shower of dust and worse billowed into the choking air.

Slowly I reached over and picked up the empty dish lying on the rancid blanket.

'See this plate?' I said. 'I named it Hunger. My knife is called Starving. I'm the only one who can eat around here, so I thought that would be fitting. My goblet is called Thirst. Bit of a joke, really, because I can wait all day for it to be filled . . .'

Freya shrugged.

'Do you like my bed hangings?' I said. I was trying to think of things to talk about, but I am not practised at this. I was starting to regret calling her back. A hero she might well be, but what was that to me?

Freya shrugged again. Clearly, she wasn't feeling very talkative.

'I went through so many names for them,' I said. I fingered what remained of the black-and-silver fabric, covered in a cheery scene of decomposing corpses dangling from gibbets. 'Rickets. Glittering Pain. Shining Harm. Shimmering Torment. They've been Glimmering Misfortune now for ages. I might rename them again in the next hundred years or so.'

'That'll be fun,' said Freya.

I looked at her with ice-dead eyes.

'Are you laughing at me?'

'No,' said Freya. 'I like naming things too. I even

named all my stuffed toys when I was little. I called my dog Bel Gazou.'

'I called mine Garm,' I said. 'That means rag. He's huge and ugly. Everything here is ugly.'

'You're not ugly,' said Freya.

I snorted.

'Not ugly? Are you blind? I'm a monster.'

The young girl shook her head.

'You know,' said Freya, 'if you tied back your hair, you'd look quite pretty.'

'Pretty?' I said. 'What's pretty?'

'It means . . . you look good,' said Freya.

I stared at her. 'How would I know?'

'Look,' Freya fumbled with her unruly curls and took off the tortoise-shell clip. 'May I touch your hair?'

I started as if Freya had asked if she could brand me.

'You want to . . . touch me?' I said.

'Well, your hair . . . I was going to . . .' Freya stopped in confusion. Maybe she thought she'd drop dead if she touched me. Maybe she would.

'We both have Medusa hair,' said Freya.

'Who's Medusa?' I said. I didn't think there was anyone named Medusa down here.

'A monster from the Greek myths,' said Freya. 'She turned people to stone if they looked at her. She had snakes for hair.'

Great. The M word again. I saw Freya bring her hand to her mouth as she realised what she'd said.

I spat. 'A monster? People always like monsters in stories.'

'I thought you'd be old and ugly,' said Freya.

'I am old and ugly,' I said. 'I'm a rotting corpse.'

'Not all of you,' said Freya. 'When you tie back those curls you'll look quite pretty.'

Freya fumbled in her pocket. She pulled out some bits of rubbish, a feather, some nuts, and then a shiny, round silver box, brighter than anything I had ever seen before.

Freya gazed at the burnished little pot wistfully for a moment.

'Put this on,' said Freya.

I raised myself onto my elbow.

'What is it?' I asked. 'A jewel? Magic?'

'It's called lip gloss,' said Freya. 'It will make your mouth shine.' She opened the round pot and handed me the gloss. I held it up to the candle, marvelling how the light bounced off the polished surface.

'I like shine,' I said. Then I gasped.

'There's – there's someone in here,' I whispered, pointing to a face in the tiny round glass.

'That's you,' said Freya.

'Me?' I said. '*Me?*' I gazed at my reflection, myself and not myself. It can't be ... I look ... I look ... ' I raised my hands to my face and touched it, staring at myself in the mirror. For the first time, I saw my pink cheeks and ice eyes, my curly silver hair.

'This is a great wonder, to see yourself so clearly.' I stuck out my tongue. The girl in the glass mirrored me. She really, truly, was me. I wasn't some ironwood hag. I wasn't troll spawn.

'Dip your finger in the gloss and smear it on your lips,' said Freya.

I almost dropped the looking glass.

'You first,' I hissed. 'I don't want to be poisoned.'

Freya smeared her finger with pink gloss and rubbed it on her mouth. I copied her. Then I looked at myself and smiled. Now my lips matched my cheeks.

Freya was right. I did not look monstrous.

'A new you,' said Freya.

She would want it back. My fingers gripped the pot. I longed for this magic more than any gift.

'Keep it,' said Freya.

I could not stop gazing at my face. I dipped my fingers in the pot and smeared the gloss on my cheeks.

'I'm sorry,' said Freya. 'It must be horrible being here.'

'It is,' I said. 'It's Hel.'

I gazed at the lip gloss. I decided in that moment.

40

SICKBED

‘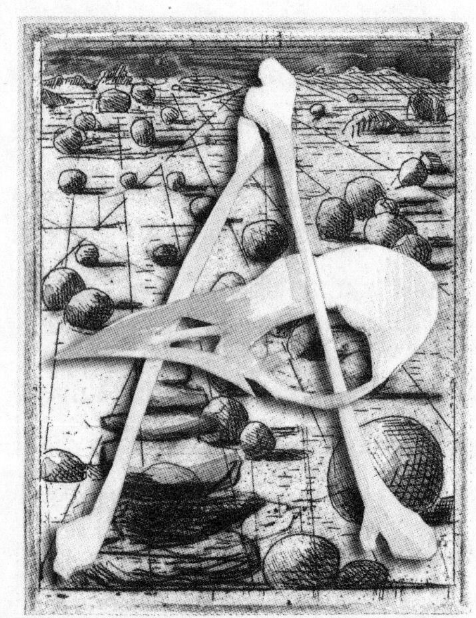 GREAT GIFT LIKE this deserves recompense,’ I said. ‘Ganglot. Fetch the *eski* under my bed.’

We sat in silence, waiting the long while for my servant to complete her task.

Freya took the wooden box from Ganglot and opened it. Her hands were shaking. Perhaps she thought I’d handed her a box of entrails, or a septic toe . . .

Then she saw the nut. She gripped the *eski* tightly and swallowed. Then she turned to me and the joy on her face exploded around me. I have never been looked at like that. No one sees me and feels joy. That look I also tucked away, to feel its spark forever.

'I'm doing this for you,' I said. 'Not for them. I hate the gods. I'll always hate them. But my revenge can wait until the Axe Age and the Wind Age and the Wolf Age at the bitter End of Days.'

'I'll build a shrine to you,' said Freya.

'That will be a first,' I said. 'Don't think you'll get too many worshippers.'

'Goodbye,' said Freya. 'Thank you. I'll never forget you.'

'Stay,' I said. 'You'll never make it back to Asgard alive. You're already ivory up to your neck. Here you can live forever. Just think, mortal Freya, life everlasting. Your friends and family will all be here to join you soon enough.'

Freya hesitated.

'This place isn't so bad once you get used to it,' I said, slowly sitting up. 'Everyone's here, you know. All the greats. You can meet anyone you like. There's no pain. No suffering.'

I was offering her immortality – of a sort.

'I can't,' said Freya. 'I have to try.'

What was I thinking? Of course she wouldn't want to stay.

'Go, then,' I said. 'See if I care.'

Freya slipped through the bed hangings onto the threshold and went back into the hall. There was the mad flutter of wings, a snarl of rage, then thundering hooves.

I heard my father bellow, 'I'll soon be picking apart your carrion!'

He continued cursing as the sound of wings grew fainter and fainter. The bird girl had escaped.

Of course I regretted it immediately. Why did I do it? I held vengeance in my power. All I had to do was to let Freya leave empty-handed. Soon the gods would have been dead and gone. The vengeance I had waited for so long was shimmering and winking at me.

Why did I give Freya the nut? I've asked myself this question over and over.

Because she gave me a gift unlike any other? Because she didn't see a monster?

Or was it to spite my father, whom I never saw again, though I heard his screams when the gods finally caught and bound him.

Maybe.

Maybe it was because I saw myself for the first time.

Maybe because I saw myself in her?

There is nothing else now but the waiting. Nothing else. I will decay here in the darkness through the slow *tick tock* to Ragnarok and the fated ending.

My saga is drawing to a close. I am locking my word hoard. Mortals, read the Testament of Hel I have set down. Tell it to your children, and your children's children.

I blow out the candle, close my eyes, lie back on my bed, and I wait for the Axe Age and the Sword Age. The

Wind Age and the Wolf Age.

I'm glad that one day Fenrir will swallow the sun and sprinkle the heavens with blood. I'm glad he'll kill Odin. I'm glad Jor will kill Thor.

Till then I'll rot on my putrid bed, till the bitter stars drop from the sky and the waters once again swallow the earth.

PART 5
Epilogue

41

RAGNAROK: THE DOOM OF THE GODS

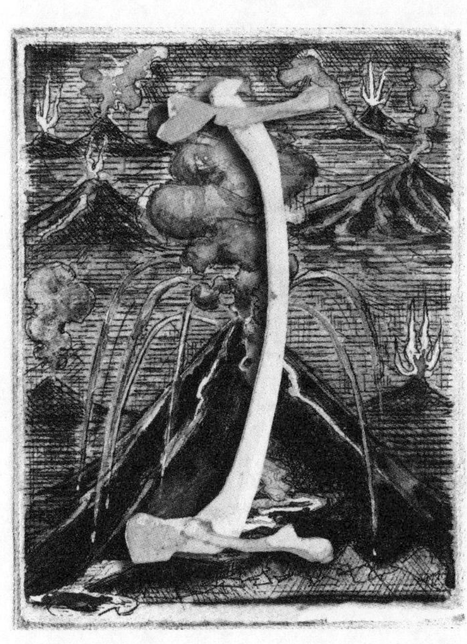

HAVE BEEN ASLEEP. I have been asleep as long as time. And then I wake. A poem an ancient skald recited to me long ago echoes in my head as I feel the worlds shifting.

Some say the world will end in fire,
Some say in ice.
From what I've tasted of desire
I hold with those who favour fire.
But if it had to perish twice,
I think I know enough of hate
To know that for destruction ice
Is also great
And would suffice.

Corpses pour down from Midgard, tsunamis of the dead. I let them speak. An avalanche of frantic ghosts, jabbering about hard frosts, winds, floods, drifting snow. Biting winters. So much slaughter, so many wars. Mountains crumbling and crashing down, seas gushing forth and spewing over the lands.

I dare not hope.

I hear the battle horn booming, echoing through the worlds.

I hear three cocks crow. One in Asgard. One in

Jotunheim. And one in Niflheim, rust red, rousing the gods, the giants, and the dead to battle, and I know the End of Days is here.

The End of Days.

I shout for my servants. I haven't spoken for so long that I have no voice.

The world tree Yggdrasil shudders and shakes, then a jagged crack like a thunderbolt wrenches apart the wailing tree while the worlds quake and all bonds break.

I hear Fen howl in victory as his fetters snap. I hear Jor thrashing out of the overflowing ocean, blowing poison through the air and the water, hear the waves rear up to the skies and flood Midgard as Jor writhes in his fury, splashing venom.

All the monsters, the forces of chaos, are let loose. The dragon crawls out of the swamp, tail whipping, hungry for blood.

My dog, Garm, the bellowing untrainable wolf-dog, roars. Garm, who'd rip out my heart given the chance. I think, *he is barking to save me, to make me leave, to remind me, GO GO. Get out before the flames*. I hear his chains snapping, his mad howling echoing as he races from his cave to join the battle.

The walls of my hall start to fissure and crack. Fire blazes out of Surt's kingdom as the giant demon rides forth, Asgard-bound, the blast of scorching smoke and the crackle of embers everywhere in his burning wake.

I shout again for my servants. Still no one comes.

I must go. It's happening and I'm not ready.

I drag my useless legs into the shaking hall. No restless ghosts. No hissing snakes. Just the roar of walls toppling and crashing around me, of benches sliding and tables splitting. My fortress walls collapse; my great iron gates shriek as they clatter to the ashy ground.

I catch a glimpse of Baldr, Nanna, as they flee.

Baldr.

Hel has emptied. I see the last to leave, my seeress mother, rising from her grave mound to join the army of the dead.

I've been left behind.

The dead have gone, mad for vengeance. The corpses over whom I reigned for so long have obeyed the cock's summons and sailed off in a ship made from dead men's nails to join the spear-clash in Asgard as the gods make their final futile stand.

Fen's jaws will gape so wide they will touch both the heavens and the earth. He will swallow One-Eye with those jaws before Odin's son Vidar rips him in two. I suddenly remember Vidar trying to play with Fen in Asgard.

I have outlived the one who banished me to Niflheim.

My banishment is over.

But I don't have time to gloat as my quaking kingdom dissolves around me.

I stagger through Eljudnir's ruins, stepping through the rubble and smashed stones and the crushed bodies of snakes. Great billowing clouds of savage smoke engulf me.

Niflheim has become a furnace. I smell burning cinders, watch ash raining down like clouds of flaking skin.

I am free to go. I am free to go.

I leave everything.

Soot covers the precipices and valleys, fluttering like a shower of burnt stars. I'm walking through the funeral pyre of my world.

I approach the Echoing Bridge, still glowing in the smoky gloom, but glowing with embers now, as a stream of molton gold rains into the river below. Modgud isn't there. She's vanished, along with everyone else. Modgud. I'd forgotten about her. It's strange how someone living can just fade from your mind, as if they've withered and died.

The river hisses and sparks. The water is alight, and a wall of fire blocks the fog road.

I wait a moment on my side, because I want to hold the thought of freedom in my mind. Just in case I'm wrong, and One-Eye's magic outlives his death and I remain trapped here.

I am too scared to move. What if –

I'm like a hawk freed from a cage, a wolf cub freed from a trap. I can't believe the door is open; I want to stay and bite.

I put out my hand and touch the glowing railing. It's hot, so hot. But I've touched it.

And nothing holds me back as I set my foot on the smoking bridge for the first time. My stumbling steps stomp and echo. I can't breathe.

I quicken my pace until I am lurching across. I'm suddenly frightened that I won't make it. I totter, grip the melting railings to heave myself over. I've never felt such panic. If Nidhogg were tracking me, I don't think I could have felt more fear.

Leaping flames barricade the exit, hissing and snapping. I won't be stopped: I walk through them.

My legs are on fire.

And then I reach through the blaze onto the other side, gasping and choking. I beat down the flames, roll on the ground.

I've escaped.

The long fog road back to the world of the living lies before me.

I don't look back. I have a memory of someone who looked behind him and . . . and . . .

The memory is gone. *Too bad for him*, I think.

I stumble up the fog road, climbing through the deepest, darkest valley, now fire, now ice, pockets of rustling embers lighting my path. My feet slosh through the ash like melted snow.

There's no rush. Even if I wanted to, I couldn't run. There's a whooshing in my ears, and I realise it's silence. The empty burnt-out kingdom of death falls behind me with every step.

Tears keep springing to my eyes, and I wipe them away. My legs tingle and ache. I am not used to movement. But I won't stop. The stink of burning keeps wafting up, even here.

My enemies are all dead. What I longed for, hoped for, waited for, has happened.

How do I feel?

Empty.

I've spent an eternity hating. I am bitter and toxic

with hatred. I search for the hate within myself, and I find it has gone. I start to cry. I never, ever, cry. Not since the first moments when I arrived in Niflheim, not since Baldr rejected me. But now that I have started, it's as if all the tears that have been dammed up inside me are pouring out.

Great gulping sobs burst from my belly.

I have lived an eternity of hating, and for what? Hate has ruled me, gnawed me. I spent eternity lying on a stinking bed. Sunk into myself, plotting and moaning and … dying. The greatest skalds and poets and musicians and thinkers were mine and what did I do? Nothing. I bewailed my bad fate. I loved so desperately, so terribly, and I let that love devour me.

Where did all that love go? All that hate?

What was I thinking?

I am two halves, life and death. And I chose death.

I thought it was love that moved me. Whatever I felt wasn't love. I know that now.

42

BRAVE NEW WORLD

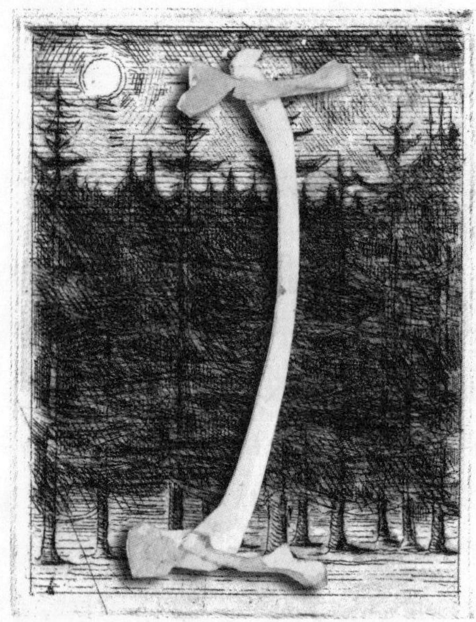

LOST COUNT OF the nights I spent struggling up the fog road. One of your years is my eye-blink. Time is different for me. Always was. Always will be.

What will I find when I finally reach the top? Would Midgard be as burnt as Niflheim?

Will there be a sun? A moon? Am I passing from one grave mound into another?

I have been walking through pitch dark. Even with my goddess eyes, I can barely see one foot in front. Occasional sparks illuminate the road, like dying stars.

And then it seems to me that I can see two feet ahead. Then three, then four.

The closer I get to the top the more light I see. Faint glimmers of soft, shining light.

A new sun has risen to replace the old.

I heave my body faster and trip over Garm's broken chains, rusting on the ground. I pick myself up and press on until I emerge at last from the cave into sunshine. Great golden sheets of sunshine.

My legs buckle, and I collapse, drunk with light.

I breathe fresh air, so sweet in my graveyard lungs. I breathe and breathe as if I cannot get enough. I'm dizzy with air, intoxicated by its crisp tang. Everywhere there are signs of fire and flood: scorched earth, blasted and toppled trees, seaweed, dead fish, shells, driftwood. And yet there are flashes of green, tiny buttons of moss pushing their way out of the blackened ground. And red poppies, flecked with ash. In the distance I see the careless ocean, retreated back to its basin.

I sit up, stretch out my shaking legs, lift my face to the red-orange sky. Floating above the acrid reek of burning is the scent of new grass. And –

Something has changed.

I don't smell me.

My legs are still withered, but I don't stink any more. And beneath the charred skin I see – a flash of pink.

Now I smile.

I am the last of the giants. I am the last of the gods. I am destruction and creation, death and life. Daughter of a giant. Daughter of a god.

Death has ambushed everyone else. The Nine Worlds are empty.

A shadow crosses the sky. I look up and see the shining serpent, Nidhogg, flying over the plain, carrying corpses from the Last Battle.

I'll deal with him.

His corpse days are done.

In fact, I think death is done. I will banish death. I am the last goddess and it's down to me to remake the world.

The old gods didn't know how to create a better world. They couldn't change their story.

Can I?

I don't know. But I can do better than One-Eye. I won't be hurling *anyone* into Niflheim for a start.

Asgard is burnt-out, empty, corpse-strewn, and I don't want to live there. I am a mountain-dweller, and that's where I'll go.

I will strive to do better with my new world. I have never created anything but I can try.

I see two fallen trees, an ash and an elm, their roots ripped from the earth. I raise them, first one, then the other, and slowly, clumsily, begin to carve.

ACKNOWLEDGEMENTS

You never know where you're going to get a good idea. The first sentence of this novel came to me on the New York subway, and I instantly heard Hel's cool, sarcastic, funny, adolescent voice. Once I realised that the Norse Goddess of the Dead was a child like her brothers, then I knew I had a story. I've never written in the first person before, and I loved it.

As always, I'd like to thank the teams at Faber and Profile, especially Andrew Franklin, Stephen Page, Leah Thaxton, Alice Swan, Hannah Love and Will Steele. (And my extraordinary illustrator, Olivia Lomenech Gill, who has exceeded my wildest dreams in the beauty and depth of her drawings.) Many armfuls of thanks to Steven Butler, my dear friend and on-call book doctor, who has yet to find a plot problem he can't solve. My husband, Martin Stamp, is a thoughtful, forensic reader, who could give up the day job to become an editor, while

Dr Mary Clayton is always game to answer any questions, however absurd.

For myth enthusiasts, H. R. Ellis Davidson's PhD thesis *The Road to Hel: A Study of the Conception of the Dead in Old Norse Literature* (Greenwood Press) could have been written to order for this book; as always I find all her books incredibly illuminating and insightful. John Lindow's *Norse Mythology: a guide to the gods, heroes, rituals and beliefs* (Oxford University Press) was an invaluable reference work. I'd also like to thank my stand-by Icelandic scholar Dr Emily Lethbridge for recommending Lotte Motz's article 'Giants in Folklore and Mythology', which was a great help in untangling several traditions about giants and their tortured relations with the gods.